happenings

katie cobb

HarperTrophy®

AN IMPRINT OF HarperCollinsPublishers

Acknowledgments

Many thanks to Antonia Markiet, for walking me through the pains of growing from writer to author; to Casey Burchby and Kathryn Silsand, for adding the final touches; and to all at HarperCollins who helped pull this book together.

Many thanks to my lunch bunch, Donna Fester, Karen Kling, and Janice Lambert, for listening to my ideas—both good and bad.

Many thanks to my writers' club, the NC/NE Texas Chapter of SCBWI, for the monthly shot of hope.

Many thanks to Mary Howington, for her enthusiastic search through the library shelves for the small details that made writing fun, and to Peggy Kennedy, for the late-afternoon talks.

Many thanks to Vicki Clark, Wanda McNeill, and Linda Rodgers, for believing that I could.

Many thanks to my family—Bob, Melody, Vincent, Bill, Gina—for sharing the journey.

And finally many, many thanks to all the students I've taught throughout the years who have given me both inspiration and joy.

Harper Trophy® is a registered trademark of HarperCollins Publishers Inc.

Happenings
Text copyright © 2002 by Linda Powley

Library of Congress Cataloging-in-Publication Data
Cobb, Katie.
Happenings / by Katie Cobb.
p.   cm.
Summary: A high school girl faces pressure from her older brother, who is also her guardian, when she and her peers peacefully protest a teacher who they believe has stopped doing her job.
ISBN 0-06-447232-9 (pbk.) — ISBN 0-06-028928-7 (lib. bdg.)
[1. Teachers—Fiction.   2. Brothers and sisters—Fiction.   3. High Schools—Fiction.   4. Schools—Fiction.]   I. Title.
PZ7.C6325Hap 2002   200124603
[Fic]—dc21   CIP
                                                                    AC

Typography by Andrea Vandergrift
❖
First Harper Trophy Edition, 2002
Visit us on the World Wide Web!
www.harperteen.com

To my brother, Bert, for giving me wings to fly

Contents

1

stirrings

"Kelsey Gene Blackwell! You're crazy if you go through with this."

Kelsey stared at her friend Marti Lawrence and said nothing. Clearly this was an argument she was not going to win, so why bother?

"Russ'll kill you," Marti pressed. "And so, for that matter, will Elliot."

Kelsey blinked, trying to hide her frustration. Her brother Russell she could handle, even if he was her guardian and took his responsibilities *way* too seriously. She'd just have to make sure he never heard about today. But Ms. Elliot would freak if she found out one of her seniors, one of her starters, walked into English class and willfully chose to do absolutely nothing.

"She'll get in your face and make you run bases until you think—"

"Back off." Kelsey exploded, forgetting that the argument was already lost. "These are my friends. What do you want me to do?"

Marti jumped on the opening. "They may be your friends, Kelsey Gene, but this isn't right. You can't up and decide one day to stop doing what the teacher asks. That's not how it works."

"But Mrs. Delaney is wrong," Kelsey insisted. "It's an advanced placement class, and time is running out. We've all signed up for the AP tests, and if we pass, we can skip freshman English next year. But how can we do that if we don't know sh—" Kelsey caught herself. No use getting Marti more riled. "The stuff?" she finished.

"Come on, KG. You've made As in English since kindergarten. You'll ace the test."

"That's not the point."

"Then what is?"

Kelsey inhaled deeply, calming herself. She didn't like Marti's attitude, but neither did she like the feeling of her own swelling temper.

"Look," she said, forcing her tone to stay neutral, "it isn't fair. In the fall Mrs. Delaney was really great. She said the work we did was like the first year of college, and trust me, it was tough. We had forty-minute writings at least twice a week, and she was constantly challenging us to think. We were reading two books a month—hard ones—and the discussions were, well, great. Now all we get are work sheets, more and more work sheets. She hardly opens her mouth, and we certainly don't say anything because if we don't finish, she marks us down. I don't know why she's changed, but if she isn't going to teach, like she's paid to do, then why should we cooperate?"

"Because you are the student, and she is the teacher. You don't run the class. She does."

"Well, we are changing all that today." Kelsey spun away, ending her part of the conversation. Hanging around listening to someone overreact was only going to make her late. She still had to stop by her locker, get her books, her homework—

No, wait. Everyone in the class had agreed: Do no work; turn in no assignment until Mrs. Delaney started really teaching again.

"Then I don't want to hear it when Russ grounds you for life," Marti called loudly to her back. "Not one word."

Two passing sophomores, members of the junior varsity team, turned to stare, and Kelsey shook her head. Marti'd just have to get over it.

Like Russ? And Elliot?

Kelsey sighed. Yeah. They'd get over it, about as

fast as Santa Claus came on December 26. She glanced at a hall clock and picked up her pace. She definitely didn't want to be the last one into class, not today. She wanted to be in place and settled when the protest began, following Drew's lead, because at lunch that was what they'd all agreed to do.

And who died and left him in charge? Kelsey asked herself. Did it matter?

Not anymore. The time to object had been thirty minutes ago, when the idea of the protest first began, not now, after everyone had agreed. Like it or not, she was committed.

"Hey, girl! Hurry up."

Ratasha Harris, a longtime friend and teammate, was waiting at the foot of the stairs. "You and Marti okay?"

Kelsey shrugged. What a silly question. Ratasha had been with them at lunch, and Marti certainly hadn't hidden her objection.

"What do you think about all this?" Kelsey asked, taking two steps at a time.

Ratasha followed close behind. "I think this class is going to be a trip, man."

Kelsey opened her mouth to say something, anything, like maybe they were moving too fast, maybe they should think things out a bit more, but stopped

4

when they stepped through the door. Drew, in his customary desk at the front of the room, was sitting, back erect, hands folded, eyes locked straight ahead. And, as agreed, the others sat equally unengaged. The protest had begun.

Quickly Kelsey took her seat at the back and assumed the same position, sitting bolt upright, hands folded in the middle of her desk. She found a spot on the board and let her eyes gently unfocus. All she wanted to do was survive for the next fifty-five minutes. Then, once Mrs. Delaney got the message that they wanted a change, it would be class as normal again.

At least that was what Kelsey hoped. But somewhere deep down an alarm was sounding, warning, insisting that she yield to her better judgment. And as it grew louder and louder, screaming for attention, Kelsey mentally reached out and shut it down.

After all, this was only one English class in the middle of a string of others. She always did her work. Always. What harm could possibly come from joining with a protest for just one day?

2

day one

Seconds after the bell Mrs. Delaney rushed though the front door and worked her way to the back, picking a path around backpacks and long legs, using the side of her loafer to scoot Terrance's notebook under his desk.

I wonder when she'll notice, Kelsey thought. To be joined with others in a collective stand felt exciting, but Mrs. Delaney seemed to be a sensitive person. Had anyone considered that she might feel hurt?

Kelsey heard a rustle of papers, and her sympathy disappeared. She didn't even have to turn around to know that this class had begun like all recent ones. Mrs. Delaney had entered the room and walked straight to her station in the back, picked up the dreaded stack from the upper-left-hand corner of her desk, and started distributing her boring assignment, sending papers and more papers of monotonous questions up each aisle. "Please read the following passage

6

and select the correct answer for each multiple-choice question. Do the following sentence completions, analogies, vocabulary exercises."

Kelsey was sick of the same routine, day after day, week after week. What was wrong with Mrs. Delaney anyhow? Why the change? No more prodding discussions and spirited debates; no more challenging essays. All she assigned anymore were grammar exercises and reading passages and questions, questions, questions. Talk about dull.

In fact, the work looked like the same type of stuff Kelsey did when she took an SAT prep class. Only they weren't preparing for the SAT; they were signed up to take the AP test, the *advanced placement* test. So how were the SAT exercises helping?

Last week, when Drew complained, Mrs. Delaney had flushed and told him if he didn't like the way she ran the class, she'd be happy to write him a pass to the counselor so he could get his schedule changed. Of course it was a bogus option. Mrs. Delaney taught the only senior AP English class, so if he wanted the weighted credit, which would boost his grade point average, he had to stick it out.

Today it took less than three minutes for the correct number of pages to be distributed. There were five assignments in all: a grammar exercise, a vocabulary drill, a set of analogies, and two long reading passages with questions. As usual Mrs. Delaney was settled behind her desk, attendance taken, assignment given, in under five minutes.

Seconds later Kelsey heard the swishing of a moving skirt followed by a soft shuffle. She ached to know what was happening, but she didn't dare turn around. Like everyone else, she sat still, hands folded on top of the work sheets stacked neatly in the center of her desk. She felt, more than saw, her teacher's gaze wandering around the room. Finally Mrs. Delaney spoke.

"Okay. Someone tell me what is going on."

Drew was ready for his five minutes of fame. "We're having a sit-in, protesting until you start teaching us like you did last semester."

"E-e-excuse me?" Mrs. Delaney sputtered. "*You're* telling *me* what to do?"

Kelsey chanced a quick glance. Mrs. Delaney's usual calm expression had taken on a sharp edge, like someone trying hard to regain control.

"This isn't a democracy," she said, color invading her cheeks. "Get to work."

No one moved.

Slowly Mrs. Delaney started walking, hands stuffed deep in her pockets, up one aisle, down another, until finally she stopped beside JJ's desk.

"Javier, do you agree with this?" she asked, touching his back.

JJ's neck reddened as he nodded.

"Ratasha," Mrs. Delaney said, moving over an aisle, "you've always prided yourself on your independence. Do you agree with this?"

"Yes, ma'am," came the soft response. "We want you to, you know, teach us like you did last semester."

"Well, you know what?" Mrs. Delaney said, addressing the whole class. "How I teach is my business, and yours is to get to work. Now." Her words rushed into the air, demanding attention, but nobody moved.

"Whatever," Mrs. Delaney mumbled, returning to her desk. "The assignment is due at the end of the period."

Five minutes down; fifty to go.

An unwelcomed sense of isolation seeped into Kelsey's heart, even though she was sitting in a room full of people. She took a deep breath and hunkered down for the duration. Her hands were jittery, her heart racing. She wanted out.

Then why don't you get up and leave?

Right, she answered herself. *Then I'd get written up for a cut, and Russell would have a fit.* She frowned deeply at that thought. She hated being accountable to anyone, let alone a thirty-one-year-old sibling, but like it or not, their dad's will had clearly appointed Russ guardian. And she had no doubt that her law-abiding brother would expect her to maintain a standard of conduct that did not include taking part in a sit-in.

As if it is any of his business, she told herself as her eyes roamed over the heads of her classmates, all staring forward, hands folded, idle. That was one advantage of sitting near the back—she could at least look around.

She'd never seen Terrance so still. Usually he was stretching his back or crossing his legs or any of a dozen other things in an effort to find comfort in a world built too small for his six-foot-six frame. His mother would be about as pleased as Russ if she knew what was going on. Kelsey closed her eyes and grinned at the imaginary conversation.

"Boy, you'd better pick up that pen and get to work. I didn't scratch my way through night school to watch you throw away your life." Then she'd stand there with her hands on her hip and ask, "Do you hear me?"

Ms. Jackson expected her son to use and expand what she saw as his greatest asset: his mind. Terrance's view was more pragmatic. He loved basketball, and his mother allowed him to play only if he brought home As. So he did.

Kelsey's smile broadened more at the mental image of Terrance—muscular, self-assured, headstrong—frantically grabbing his pen and going to work under his mother's fierce gaze. JJ said Terrance's greatest talent was his ability to blend with a team and strengthen the whole. "Smooth" was the word JJ used, though the only thing Kelsey knew was that she liked watching Terrance play.

On the flip side, JJ said he most respected Kelsey for her calm, logical mind, and then he'd laugh uproariously. No one who knew Kelsey would agree with such a description. It would be like calling a lioness a lamb.

Her eyes shifted slightly and found JJ's back. One of the most popular students on campus, JJ—Javier Juarez—was into everything. He played trombone in the band, soccer on the weekends, and was president of the Student Council. He was treasurer of the Science Club and volunteered as a student translator—that is, when he wasn't working. He spent almost twenty hours a week helping his dad in their family-owned auto shop, something he enjoyed almost as much as geology. JJ's dream was to open a jewelry store, maybe with a partner, one who could handle the business end while JJ dealt with the gems.

If he gets to go to college.

What a sobering thought. JJ's family was huge, seven brothers and sisters, and his best chance of continuing his education was pinned squarely on winning a scholarship. Even though he didn't seem as intense as some of the guys she knew, JJ had an inward determination that bordered on obsession. For him, testing out of freshman English wasn't just a lark; it was a financial perk he couldn't afford to lose.

Kelsey's attention moved on to Ratasha, who, like the others, sat erect with eyes straight ahead. JJ said she was one fine-looking woman, but she ignored him the way she did everyone who flattered and teased. She didn't want to be derailed with sweet talk and promises because she wanted to make a difference. She was proud of her heritage, her culture, and it bothered her to hear others speak glibly of Martin Luther King in terms of a holiday or of Malcolm X as an excuse for disruption. She planned to major in education to be sure that the next generation understood the meaning behind those great leaders' words.

Again Kelsey scanned the room. How much time had passed? Ten minutes? Fifteen? Shoulders were now sagging, and occasionally a head drooped forward. Fifty-five minutes was a long time to do nothing. Had Drew considered that?

Probably not. Perhaps the most intelligent of the group, he had little ambition. Russ's word for Drew was "spoiled," and while she hated to side with her brother, in some ways Kelsey agreed. Once Drew's parents had caught him smoking pot and told him they were disappointed.

Disappointed? What a deal! If Kelsey's father had caught her with pot, he would definitely have done more than tell her he was "disappointed." She wasn't sure exactly what, but he'd had a way of coming up with creative punishments that, as he said, "fit the crime." So she'd probably have had to work in a methadone clinic, or do research on the effects of pot on the brain, or sit through the sentencing of a convicted drug user.

Russ, though, she could predict. As a state trooper he had no problems meting out consequences. He'd simply ground her for eternity, and then turn her over to their middle brother, Nathan. In his second year of medical school, Nathan had a way of getting into Kelsey's head and making her really think. It was he, not her father or Russ, who had convinced her never to do drugs. With Russ married and their mother "away," Nathan was the only other one still at home, though with his schedule he was rarely around. Sometimes Kelsey missed life as it had been, as it was before her father died, before her mother got sick. She missed having a father around who would do more than "disapprove" if he caught her smoking, though that was all Drew's parents had done.

The good news was that after staying stoned once for nearly a month, Drew had sobered up on his own. He wanted to be a writer, and he used this as an excuse to do crazy, unacceptable things, supposedly to fill up his "well of personal experience." Once he'd even asked Kelsey to go to bed with him so that he'd know what it was like to take a virgin. She'd told him to go to hell. If she wanted—

The sound of the bell brought a stirring of relief as weary backs relaxed and stiff legs flexed. With exaggerated precision Drew gathered his papers into a careful pile, one page, two. When all five were stacked, crisp and neat, he walked to the back of the room and laid them on Mrs. Delaney's desk. She didn't even glance up. One by one the others did the same, crisscrossing the sets so that each remained separate. Kelsey stared in mute surprise at the regulated performance. It was as if they'd rehearsed! Still she followed along too, more hurried than most, anxious not to be the last one caught in the room.

And suddenly it was over. Kelsey rushed through the crowded hall, weaving in and out, down the stairs, to the right. Lockers slammed; voices swelled; everything was the same, like yesterday. Right?

Wrong. Yesterday she hadn't just taken part in a

sit-in, refusing to work. Yesterday she had simply done her assignment, turned it in, and walked on to her next class.

Surely tomorrow Mrs. Delaney would go back to the way she used to teach. Once she'd had a chance to think things over, she'd come around.

But what if she didn't?

Kelsey felt an uneasy emptiness settle deep in her stomach. She'd seen the backslaps as she left the room, heard Drew bragging about how tomorrow would be even better.

Tomorrow?

Wasn't it supposed to be a one-day protest? Something to get Mrs. Delaney's attention?

Even if he didn't like it, Russ would probably understand why Kelsey initially joined her friends, but he'd never agree that a second day or third day was necessary. She hated it when he fussed at her, just hated it. But if the protest continued, she'd have to stick.

Maybe Mrs. Delaney will get the message and start teaching like she used to, Kelsey thought, settling in for her last class, but the words had a hollow ring. Mrs. Delaney hadn't reacted at all as they'd expected.

Again the alarm sounded, the one deep in her head, warning, and again Kelsey shut it off, pushing it back where it could no longer be heard. After all, there was nothing she could do, not really, not until after their next class, after Mrs. Delaney had had a chance to think things through.

No use worrying about what hasn't happened, she told herself. Tomorrow would come soon enough.

3

first warning

Kelsey sat at a four-way stop, trying to summon enough courage to go on. She could turn right, instead of left, or go straight, any direction other than toward the Lawrences' house.

How had she ever let Marti talk her into this?

"Because she snuck up on you," Kelsey said to herself, taking her foot off the brake. One minute she and Ratasha had been talking to their teammates about the protest, and the next she was accepting an invitation to join Marti and her dad for dinner. It was halfway through practice—when Kelsey was trying to figure out why Marti hadn't fussed more—that it hit home. She was going to tell her dad about what happened at school.

Actually, though Kelsey'd never admit it out loud, the idea was a good one. As principal of the junior high Dr. Lawrence would be able to offer sound advice. The downside was he'd been one of her own father's closest friends, and he was as determined as Russ to see that Kelsey turned out right.

Three minutes later she pulled into Marti's drive and smiled at Jim Lawrence, hunched over an upturned lawn mower, struggling to loosen a bolt. His head rose at the sound of the unfamiliar engine, but curiosity quickly melted into a welcoming smile. By the time Kelsey turned off the ignition and stepped out of the car, he was standing in the garage door, wiping his hands on a shop rag.

"And to what do I owe this pleasant surprise?" he asked, pulling her toward him for a hug.

She shrugged sheepishly. "Nathan's at the library, and well, here I am."

Marti, who'd just arrived, was fast approaching, flapping a sheet of white paper high in the air as she walked.

"Better make sure that's sharp," she called, pointing to the half-installed blade. "Because you said if I got a B, you'd do the first cut of the season."

Dr. Lawrence released Kelsey and took the paper from his daughter's hand. "This I've got to see."

Even though the letter B was clearly visible on the front of the English test, he turned it over and over, blinking, rubbing his eyes as if somehow his vision had failed.

"DAAAD!" Marti fussed as he wrapped an arm around her shoulder.

"I knew you could do it."

"No, you didn't. You hate to cut the grass."

"Hmm," he mumbled thoughtfully, giving her a squeeze. "I might agree to cut it all summer if you make the A/B honor roll for the year."

Kelsey watched Marti step back and study her father carefully. His face was dead serious, but his eyes were twinkling. English was Marti's worst subject, killing her GPA. He was constantly coming up with new challenges to encourage her to work harder.

"I'd have to get an A on my junior paper."

Dr. Lawrence raised his eyebrows and nodded.

"You have time to proofread?"

The question was directed to Kelsey, who had breezed through her three years of advanced English without breaking a sweat.

"I'll make the time," Kelsey promised.

"Then okay!" Marti stuck out her hand, and she and her father sealed the deal with a shake. "Now, what's for dinner? I'm starved."

Dr. Lawrence led the way, while the girls, coming off two hours of grueling softball practice, lagged behind. He'd already poured the milk and set an extra place before they wandered through the kitchen door.

Kelsey hesitated at the familiar sight of predinner confusion. Stumbling on any sign of "normal" family life was always a shock. Normal? The way hers had been before her father had died of an aneurysm? Before her mother had gone nuts? Russ would definitely fuss if he heard that word.

Nuts. Nuts! NUTS!

She could almost hear her brother now: *Try clinically depressed, Kelsey Gene.*

Whatever. Her life had changed forever the day her father keeled over last May.

"Come back, KG," Marti said, and Kelsey gave her a slight grin. Both knew where her mind had wandered and the danger of its lingering.

"You know," Dr. Lawrence said, motioning the two toward the table, "Ruth will be disappointed to have missed you, Kelsey Gene. She has an open house tonight, so she stayed at school."

Easy conversation flowed around a meal of pepper steak, rice, Jell-O salad, and homemade rolls. Kelsey savored every bite, enjoying each taste with delicious slowness. She never ate like this anymore. She was swallowing her last mouthful, content and satisfied, when Marti got to the point.

"Dad, if Kelsey asked you for advice, would you tell Russ?"

Dr. Lawrence's clear blue eyes jumped from his daughter to her friend. "I think that would depend on whether on not I thought she was in danger. Is there something you'd like to talk about, Kelsey Gene?"

"Sort of," Kelsey answered, wondering if she would have ever broached the subject without Marti's nudge.

"Then let's go into the den, where we will be more comfortable. You two can get the dishes later."

Kelsey felt stuck to her chair. She really wasn't sure she wanted to tell Dr. Lawrence about the protest. But why? Hadn't it been the right thing to do? She rose, followed the others, and claimed the corner of the soft-cushioned sofa as hers.

"Dad, say one of the teachers at the junior high stopped teaching," Marti said, and Kelsey smiled. How like her friend to get right to the point. "And say the students decided that if she wasn't going to teach, they weren't going to work. What would you do?"

Dr. Lawrence leaned forward thoughtfully. "Exactly how has this person stopped teaching? I need specifics."

"Let's say she simply started passing out work sheets, lots and lots of work sheets," Marti answered, shifting around in her mother's overstuffed reading chair. "But she never offered any help. She just sat behind her desk all period."

"Are the work sheets self-explanatory?"

Marti frowned. "Yes."

"And are the students learning?"

"Well, they are learning how to do work sheets—grammar, and stuff like that—but the teacher never talks or helps them or anything," Marti said. "So what would you do?"

"I'd probably start by talking to the teacher, asking her about the change of methods, asking her to define her objectives and goals. But *if* the students are learning, and *if* the teacher can defend her strategies, then I would have to support her actions."

"Even if the class was AP English?"

Dr. Lawrence's eyes settled on Kelsey. "I think you'd better tell me the whole story without the hypothetical what ifs."

Kelsey took a deep breath and plunged in, beginning with lunch, when everyone decided to strike, moving on to what had happened in class, describing Mrs. Delaney's reaction and ending with Drew's hint of more to come tomorrow. As she spoke, she watched Dr. Lawrence's expression change from casual interest to deep concern. His first words were not at all what Kelsey wanted to hear.

"I don't suppose you would consider going in tomorrow and doing your work independent of the others?"

She shook her head. She'd spent the better part of the afternoon trying to understand her own motives as well as her responsibilities to her classmates. Finally she'd settled on an answer.

"It wouldn't be right," she said, for the first time testing the words out loud. "I'll probably do okay on the AP test no matter how Mrs. Delaney teaches, but what about JJ and Terrance? English is hard for them. They barely qualified for the AP class, and they need all the help they can get." Kelsey shook her head again. "No, Mrs. Delaney is wrong on this one. She's hurting their chances of passing the test, and if lending my support helps my friends, then that's what I have to do."

A hint of a smile crossed Dr. Lawrence's face. "That certainly wasn't the answer I wanted to hear, but I can tell you are your father's child."

Kelsey flushed slightly at what seemed to be a compliment.

"He could argue a point better than Daniel Webster against the devil—even when he was wrong."

Kelsey met his eyes. "I am not wrong on this."

Dr. Lawrence's laughter filled the room. "Your dad was never wrong either. At least he'd never admit it." He stopped and caught his breath. "And somehow I suspect that whether you admit it or not, you're not as sure of your position as you want me to believe."

Kelsey looked away. Were her thoughts that transparent?

"Give me a few days to check around. This sure doesn't sound like Eileen Delaney at all."

"Are you going to tell Russ?" Kelsey asked, steeling herself for his answer.

It was a long time coming. "No. But I strongly urge you to. Too many people already know what's happened, so it's just a matter of time until he hears about it from someone."

She nodded and turned toward Marti. "We'd better get started on the kitchen."

"That's okay. I'll get it," Marti said quickly. "You go on home and see if you can figure a way out of this mess."

Kelsey groaned. Marti had effectively cut off her best effort to delay, so sometime between now and class tomorrow she was going to have to really think about this protest. Dr. Lawrence was right. She wasn't as confident inside as her words sounded. In fact, she felt like a crab caught in a one-way trap.

It was as if the moment she walked into English and joined the others, a door had slammed shut behind her, and now, no matter which way she looked, there was no way out.

4

family ties

Kelsey reached for her cell phone as soon as she cleared the Lawrences' drive.

"Hey, JJ," she said when her friend answered, "want to meet at the track? My muscles are really tight, and I thought walking a bit would help stretch them out."

"Can't," he answered. "Mom and Dad are at the grocery store, and I've got the kids."

"You could bring them," Kelsey suggested. She really wanted company, but JJ groaned.

"That doesn't even sound fun. Besides, Araceli's asleep. You okay? You talk to Russ?"

Kelsey bristled. Russ, Russ, Russ. Why was everyone so worried about Russ?

"No. You talk to your dad?"

"Now why would I want to do that?" JJ replied. "I have things to do besides sit in my room."

"Wish you could meet me. I really don't want to go home. Nathan is at the library."

"And the house will be empty. How long will your mom be gone?" JJ asked gently.

"The doctor says she's making progress, but I guess she had a real break from reality. He won't give us a time period but said it could be six months or more."

"I'm sorry," JJ said. "I know it's tough being by yourself so much. Used to be so much happening at your house. I mean, we all used to hang there."

"Until Russell set down his rules," Kelsey said. "Now no one can come over unless Nathan is home, and that's like never."

"Well, you could always move in with Russ and Amy. It's not like they haven't asked."

"Right. Like that would work," Kelsey countered. "Russ is into my life enough as it is."

The sound of a distant buzzer pulled away JJ's attention. "Listen, I've got to run. I popped a pizza in the oven, and it's done. But hey, want to come over for a while?"

"No, thanks," Kelsey said. She'd already had one dose of family life with the Lawrences. Two in one night might set her back farther than she wanted to go. "See ya tomorrow."

"Stay out of trouble," JJ teased, dropping his voice almost to a whisper. "You know Big Red is watching you."

"Shut up," Kelsey said, laughing as they both hung up. No one but JJ would dare call Russ Big Red, even though between his height and bright auburn hair the description fit.

Besides, a hot bath would relax her muscles and definitely take less time than going to the track. She had so much to do: calculus and physics and creative writing, not to mention paying bills and running through a load of laundry. But at least there wouldn't be anyone around to hassle her, tell her to go to bed. She could work all night if she had to. She certainly had her freedom.

"Well, freedom isn't all it's cracked up to be," Kelsey said out loud as she stopped at a light. She wondered how many of her classmates had any idea what waited for them after graduation, if they realized that once you left high school you also left your casual, carefree days. For Kelsey it had just happened a little earlier than for most. She *knew* how easy life had been before her father died.

She turned into the parking lot of the 7-Eleven, switched the key to turn off the engine, and moved it back to engage the electrical system. The song on the

CD was a good one, and she leaned against the head-rest, listening, tapping her fingers against the steering wheel, letting the music play its magic for her soul. A little caffeine, a hot bath, and this night might not be so bad.

When the music ended, she flipped off the CD, got out, and walked stiffly into the store. She shouldn't be so tight this late into the season, but then she hadn't been working out much.

"Good evening," the clerk said when Kelsey opened the door. She nodded in acknowledgment as she headed back to the refreshment center. There she filled a large cup full of coffee, added cream and sugar, then went back to pay.

"You doing okay tonight?" the clerk asked, scanning the code for the drink while Kelsey dug into her pocket for a dollar.

"Sure am. How about you?" Even though she wasn't much in the mood for talk, the woman was only doing her job.

The clerk smiled, as if unaccustomed to having her own welfare checked, and counted out the change. "Have a good evening."

"You too," Kelsey said, stepping outside into the now-empty lot. She set the coffee on the roof of the Renegade and checked for her keys, first her left pocket, then her right, then her left pocket again.

"Oh, no," she muttered, hooding her eyes as she peered into the Jeep and saw what she knew she'd find even before she looked: her keys in the ignition, still waiting for the next song.

"I'm not believing this." Kelsey slammed her palm onto the window hard enough to rock the Renegade. How could she be so dumb? She turned around and covered her face with her hands. What now?

Call Russ, her conscience urged. *You know he won't mind.*

Kelsey's head popped back up. No, he wouldn't mind; he never did. So why did it crawl all over her to have to ask for help?

Whatever.

She had to do something. Standing out in the night air thinking about life wasn't getting her homework done.

With a sense of resignation, Kelsey grabbed her coffee and headed back into the 7-Eleven. She would need to use the store phone, rather than the pay phone, because she didn't have enough change left from the coffee to make a call. Then she would have to hang around until Russ got there, which hopefully would be fast. She hated waiting, but sometimes she didn't have a choice. Besides, she could use the time to think. Maybe she should tell him about the protest. Maybe this was fate's way of giving her the opportunity to do what she would never have done without a push.

Or maybe it was just the end to a day that had "bad" written all over it, and the worst was yet to come.

5

big red

"Hey, Kelsey Gene," Russ said, stepping down from his Ford F-150 pickup ten minutes after he'd gotten his sister's call. "You okay?"

"Yeah. I just locked my keys in the car."

"Bet that put a spin on your day."

You have no idea, Kelsey thought, watching as he fingered his ring of spares, hunting the one for the Jeep. It was hard to know how to act when you've just done something so all-fired foolish.

"I should have it opened in a second here. Did you enjoy your dinner at Jim's?"

Kelsey stiffened. "You were checking up on me?"

"No," Russ said, selecting a key and inserting it in the lock. "I called Jim about the track meet next month. I told him I'd help out, and I needed the exact date. He just mentioned you'd been by."

"Oh," Kelsey said, wondering what else Dr.

Lawrence had said. "He talked me into helping too. I think I'm working the high jump."

"He's got me running the clock for the races, but at least I'll get to see some action."

Russ twisted the key once and the lock popped free.

"Thanks," Kelsey said. "Hope you were done with supper."

"Charlie had T-ball practice, so we ate early. You sure you're okay?"

She nodded.

"Then why do you need coffee so late in the day?" he asked, looking at the half-empty Styrofoam cup sitting on the hood.

"I don't know. It just sounded good after such a full meal."

"Uh-huh," Russ said, picking up Kelsey's coffee and taking a *long* swig. "Want to tell me something?"

She lunged for the drink. "Come on, Russ. I was enjoying that."

He laughed and handed her the near-empty container. "I'd buy you some more, but Nathan would have a fit. So how are you two doing?"

"The same as we were doing yesterday when you asked, and the day before, and the day before that," Kelsey said, tossing the cup into the trash without bothering to finish it. "We *are* okay, Russ. Everything is fine."

"Uh-huh," he said. "Which is why you are drinking coffee at night and locking your keys in the car. Why don't I stop over for a while?"

"Russ, I have a ton of homework. I really need to get started on it."

"I'll stay out of your way. I could do a few chores, and then maybe we could get some ice cream or something when you wanted a break."

Funny. Less than an hour before she had desperately wanted company. Now all Kelsey could think of was how to get rid of this brother. "Let's do it later, Russ. Maybe this weekend."

Russ studied her for a long while before nodding. "Okay, but you sure there isn't something bothering you?"

Kelsey shook her head. There was, but she wasn't going to discuss everything that had happened just to satisfy her brother's intuition. She would tell him about the protest when she was ready.

He gathered her close for a hug. "Call me when you get home. Okay?"

"Russell, I'll be okay. It's only a few blocks," Kelsey protested, squeezing back hard. Hugging was a way of life with the Blackwells.

"Humor me," Russ said, moving away. He gave her back a final pat, and she nodded consent. If she didn't, he'd worry himself silly until he came over to the house to check on her, and then she'd never get anything done.

"Thanks, Russ," she called as he walked back to his truck. "I really appreciate your coming out."

"No problem. It makes me feel good that you let me help."

Kelsey watched him pull away and head out of the lot. She knew the only reason he hadn't made her leave first was that she'd promised to call.

He's coming around, her conscience chimed in. *He's trying to give you your space.*

"Yeah, right," she mumbled, still reluctant to move. "Which is why he calls me every night if I don't check in."

She reached into the Renegade and pulled out four quarters. Another cup of coffee sounded so good.

You'll never sleep if you do, she cautioned herself, and put the coins away.

"Best get on home," she added, sliding behind the wheel, and then laughed at the image of her, standing in the lot of the 7-Eleven, having a conversation with herself.

Maybe she should have mentioned the protest to

Russ, but then he *would* have come over to the house and nothing would have gotten done. He would have asked a zillion questions and wanted to get into the middle of things. She'd talk to him, but later, when she had time for a good chat, time to help him understand that she really hadn't lost her mind, after English tomorrow, when she had a better idea of where things were heading.

No need to bring any more worry into this day.

6

day two

Three zeros? Four? Five?

Kelsey sat at her desk, hands folded primly on top, eyes staring straight ahead, mind working overtime.

Ninety-three, plus one hundred, plus ninety-two, plus ninety-two, plus zero, zero, zero, zero, *zero*! Twenty percent of the grade was based on classwork, twenty percent on homework, twenty percent on quizzes, twenty percent on major tests, twenty percent on participation.

Frantically she calculated, adding, dividing, but after starting over twice, she gave up. She needed to see the numbers written down to make any sense out of the figures, though one thing was crystal clear: With all those zeros she was now failing.

Failing English?

Russell would never understand!

She glanced slowly around the room, wondering if

the others felt the same panic, if Mrs. Delaney had jolted anyone else. What if she did fail the whole class?

The thought was impossible to comprehend, especially since lunch had been a celebration of what Drew was calling a victory. The buzz about yesterday's protest had been simply electric, but Kelsey barely listened. She had a bigger worry, one she hadn't thought of before.

Why on earth would Mrs. Delaney give in when she held all the cards, a fact that became painfully apparent within minutes after the tardy bell had rung? One by one Mrs. Delaney had passed back yesterday's papers—five of them in all—each with a student's name penned neatly above the grade: zero. Then she'd called for the homework assignment and given a pop quiz.

FOLLOW DREW'S LEAD.

How Kelsey hated hearing those words! They'd become the class motto whispered over and over again as if they held some wondrous truth.

First Drew had accepted the returned papers and set them neatly on the floor, then turned the quiz in blank. It was like following a Judas goat to the slaughter. Now there would be two more zeros to add to the five.

So where to from here? Talk to Russ? No, things

had gone too far for that. Nathan? He'd be with his study group until after midnight. Russ's wife, Amy? It wasn't fair to put her in the middle. Who then? Her softball coach, Ms. Elliot? Her other teachers? The senior counselor? Mr. Arnold, the vice principal? It wasn't the lack of someone to talk to that stalled Kelsey; it was a lack of enthusiasm for what she would have to say.

So why didn't she pick up her pen and do the work, start earning back a decent grade? Because deep inside she believed in what they were doing. *She* was learning in spite of Mrs. Delaney's new approach, but she'd always been good working on her own. Her father had read to her and with her from the time she was born, instilling in his daughter a true love of the written word. But what if he hadn't? Would English still be her thing? Could she have handled silent reading and questions, day after day, over and over again? Probably not, and, since Mrs. Delaney *was* wrong, solidarity was a must. Otherwise, everyone would be lost, including Kelsey with her now-failing average.

Long after midnight, as she lay in bed, trying to forget about her miserable day, the phone rang, sending Kelsey into immediate alert.

"Hope you weren't sleeping," said a quiet voice,

and Kelsey sighed with relief. It was JJ.

"Not even close. I'd thought about taking a drive, just to clear my head."

"This late?" JJ asked. "Big Red would have a fit."

"True," Kelsey said, laughing. "So, what's up?"

"I'm really worried about this thing in English. You got any ideas?"

"None," Kelsey admitted, rolling over. "But it sure has me stressed."

"Same here. Wanta meet at Mickey D's for coffee tomorrow?"

"Can't," Kelsey answered. "Nathan left a note asking to borrow the Renegade. His truck's in the shop."

"Then I'll pick you up."

It was a good idea. Kelsey had planned to call Marti in the morning, but dawn was not her friend's best hour.

Sounds of a pained cry floated across the line, interrupting the conversation.

"It's Araceli," JJ explained, cooing softly to calm the child. "She has an earache. The doctor says she needs tubes, but my dad is self-employed. No insurance. You know how it is."

Kelsey nodded, sharing JJ's frustration, though in reality she had no idea what it was like to be in a position where pain was measured in dollars and cents.

"I could talk to Nathan," she suggested.

"No way. Dad won't take charity."

Kelsey suspected the pride she heard in JJ's voice was as much his own as his dad's. She tried a different approach. "You know, Nathan's truck is a mess. He says he doesn't have time to shop for a new one, so maybe they could trade services or something. He could find a doctor to fix Araceli, and your dad could fix Nathan's truck."

"He knows about ears?" JJ's voice was getting softer.

"He'll know someone who does. That's one of the benefits of hanging around the ER."

"Then maybe you could ask him. It isn't right that she hurts," JJ whispered. "I'm gonna put her down now. She's asleep."

"So what time tomorrow?" Kelsey asked, for some reason whispering back.

"Come on out when you're ready. I'll be waiting."

An unwanted surge of nostalgia washed over Kelsey as she hung up. How many times had Russ held her when she hurt? Soothed her when she was sick? Wakened her from a bad dream? His room had been just down the hall, and no matter how big the imaginary monsters or how real the nightmare, he'd

40

always been able to make bad things disappear.

Now he seemed to be at her all the time, fussing about this, grumping about that. *Are you getting enough rest? What did you eat for supper? Do you need any money for gas?* Why didn't he realize she could handle things on her own?

If only she were little again and life were simple and uncomplicated and fun. Damn this protest! It was spoiling the end of her senior year. If only she could turn the clock back to Tuesday, maybe she wouldn't have been so quick to follow Drew's lead. But she had, and now she had zeros, lots and lots of zeros! If only she could come up with some other solution, a better way to get Mrs. Delaney's attention, a way to make her understand.

If only . . . If only . . . *if only*!

If only it were yesterday and this were all just a bad dream.

7

first plan

It was almost two before Kelsey fell into a hard, dreamless sleep. When morning came, she rose feeling drained, puffy, dull. She ran through her morning routine with a clumsy stiffness, showering, dressing, grabbing her books. JJ was already waiting in the drive, quietly listening to a tape, when she stumbled outside. He leaned across the passenger seat and popped the door open.

"What took you so long?"

Kelsey groaned as she scooted in. "And I thought I was an early bird. I need coffee." She leaned against the headrest and closed her eyes.

JJ grinned as he swung his pride and joy, a restored 1967 maroon Ford Mustang, onto the street, threw the gearshift forward, and tore out. Kelsey didn't even flinch. JJ was a good driver, in spite of his tendency to show off. He pulled into the McDonald's lot seven minutes later with the same breakneck flourish.

"Let's eat in the car," he said, swerving around to the back and stopping by the outside speaker. "You'd be dangerous on your feet."

"Coffee," Kelsey moaned, and JJ laughed. Within minutes she was sipping the warm, rich liquid, waiting for it to jump-start her brain.

"Better?" he asked, after she'd drunk half a cup, and she nodded slightly. "You figure up your average last night?"

Kelsey nodded. "With the zeros it's sixty-seven. What's yours?"

"Fifty-three. I'm really worried, Kelsey Gene."

She sat up straighter and turned sideways in her seat. JJ used her full name so rarely it was like a call to arms.

"Maybe," he continued, staring out the front windshield while he sipped his Dr Pepper, "we could sneak our work out of the room, hide it in our notebook or something, and turn it in later. That way we wouldn't get zeros, and no one else would know."

The suggestion wiggled around Kelsey's mind until it found a fragile foothold. It would allow them to continue their show of solidarity but still maintain their averages. JJ had apparently given the idea some thought.

"What about tests?" she asked, thinking of the quiz.

"Maybe we could take them after school or something."

"Maybe," Kelsey agreed. "Have you talked to Terrance?"

"Yeah, but you know how he is. Basketball is his world. If it isn't pockmarked, round, and bouncing, he couldn't care less, if his mother doesn't find out. What about Ratasha?"

"We haven't talked much, but she likes the idea of the protest. She says passive resistance has been behind some of the best changes in history."

"Think she'll go along with us?"

Kelsey wasn't sure. She started a mental scorecard, putting those who were beginning to have doubts on one side, those who were set on following Drew on the other. So far the score was two—she and JJ—to about thirteen. Ratasha was among the undecided.

"Ever wonder what Mr. Lazoya will say when he finds out?" Kelsey asked, referring to the sponsor of the Science Club.

"He won't have to *say* a word."

Kelsey felt the same way about facing Russ. "Do *you* think Mrs. Delaney is wrong?"

JJ shrugged. "At least I was learning something with

the work sheets. Now I'm wasting my time, and the AP test isn't that far away."

"So the value of passive resistance isn't worth the sacrifice?"

"I don't know. Maybe we should be resisting our peers, and not Mrs. Delaney."

JJ's answer dug to the core of their dilemma, but until they were sure, how could they go against the others?

"So you think we should stick with the protest for a little while longer, but try to do as much as we can outside class? Isn't that kind of low? Like cheating on our friends?"

JJ shrugged. "Can you come up with something better?"

Kelsey shook her head. She didn't want to think anymore about protests and zeros and school.

"So who is your date this week?" she asked, settling into easier conversation as she watched the dawn strengthen into day.

"My mother's set me up with her friend's daughter. She tells me she has a good heart, so I *know* she's gonna be ugly!"

"A sexist's statement if I ever heard one!" Kelsey declared, and JJ's eyes widened as he pointed a finger at himself.

"Yes, *you*!" Kelsey said.

JJ frowned heavily. "Let me get this straight. You let me buy you coffee, and now you're dissing me?"

"You insult yourself, JJ. Who would you rather have for the mother of your children? A woman with a pure soul or beauty?"

"Both would be nice."

"Come on. One or the other. Choose."

"I'm not going to marry this girl, just take her out on Saturday night."

Suddenly Kelsey was too tired to argue, even in fun. She crossed her arms over her chest and turned toward the side window, giving JJ as much of her back as she could.

"Hey," he insisted, "I'm young. I have hormones."

"Which at the moment have absorbed all your good sense." Kelsey continued to stare outside. "Drive. Before I decide to walk."

"Assuming I let you stay in this car!"

Kelsey spun around, ready to fight, only to find JJ smiling.

"Just because I appreciate a pretty woman, including you," he said, tapping her nose, "doesn't mean I'm a chauvinist."

She ducked her head and wondered what was going on. A compliment? He reached over to rub her back, and suddenly she wanted to stay with him all day, someplace safe.

"As much as I'd like to continue this," he said, echoing her thoughts, "we don't want to be late." He took one last drink of the Dr Pepper and reached for the key.

Kelsey glanced at the clock on the dash. First period was still an hour away! If JJ'd been hitting on her, why had he stopped? She shot him a quizzical look.

"You do look fine this morning," he said, turning over the ignition, "but I don't want to spoil a good friendship by doing something that could cause a strain."

Immediately he slipped the car into gear, and the Mustang flew out of the lot.

And if we weren't such close friends? Kelsey wondered. It was an interesting question. She'd never thought of JJ in any other way, but she had to admit his lean, muscular body, thick dark hair, and sparkling brown eyes had appeal.

Female chauvinist pig, she chided herself, and the thought made her grin. JJ would love to hear that remark. They were always teasing, challenging each other. He was a good friend, the best, but she was too tired to consider him more. Maybe tomorrow, after she'd had some sleep.

Kelsey closed her eyes and leaned back, listening to the hum of the motor as JJ drove to school. At least they had some plan, a way to keep from failing until an agreement could be reached. Maybe today wouldn't be so bad after all. Maybe by the time it was over things would be settled and she would be sharing a good laugh with Russ about all that had happened.

But then again, it was barely past dawn.

8

day three

Kelsey felt the change even before she saw the table, stacked with neatly piled papers. Instructions on the board were bold and clear: "Pick up one packet; take it to your seat; follow all directions carefully."

Pick up? Not while the whole class was watching! Why didn't Delaney count the number of students present in each row and pass the papers up the aisles, like before?

Because she's testing you, seeing if anyone is strong enough to stand alone, Kelsey thought as she sat, hands folded, eyes straight ahead, waiting, thinking, churning—for the third day in a row. Only this time there was no work on her desk, no assignment, just her ever-present thoughts chipping away at her resolve.

Buoyed by the meeting with JJ, she found the morning had passed quietly until lunch, when excited talk of "one more day" swelled through the cafeteria din. It hadn't mattered, though, because she and JJ had their own agenda, their secret, a way to control their fate. Now they were buried even deeper in zeros than before.

Find something to focus on, Kelsey thought as she settled in for the siege.

Her father would never have believed she was actually choosing to do nothing for class after class, fifty-five minutes after fifty-five minutes, day after day, nothing but stare at the wall, twenty by twenty-five feet, head still, feet still, hands still, mind still.

She wished. But her mind wouldn't obey. Over and over it kept relaying the messages from her brain, yelling "MOVE, MOVE, MOVE."

Her whole body ached.

Try to relax, she told herself. *Start with your toes. This little piggy went to market—*

Kelsey smiled at the memory, almost a physical sensation of sitting on her father's lap, smelling his cologne, hearing him laugh. She had been what? Four? Five?

A wave of emptiness swept over her, and she wondered if the feeling would ever go away, if her brothers felt it too, if they sometimes ached with desperate anguish, knowing they would never again be completely whole.

Maybe their mother's withdrawal had certain

advantages. Maybe it blocked the pain.

Hey, Kelsey commanded herself, *forget the toes. Start at the top.*

How do you relax your hair? she asked herself.

Nathan, the only one blessed with their mother's thick dark waves, said that was why she and Russ clashed so much. They were too much alike, from their red hair to their temperaments, and it was hard to be patient with your own flaws.

Patience. That didn't come easy for Russ, though Kelsey had to admit he'd been trying lately to be open-minded. He'd come a long way since their father's death, since the time Kelsey had mentally retreated, seeking a world without pain.

Talk to me, Kelsey Gene. Now.

When either brother said that, she knew she was in for a long haul. *Talk. Now. I mean it. You're not leaving this room until you tell me what's wrong.*

At first no one recognized her withdrawal after the funeral, not even Kelsey, until the rage exploded with a will of its own, demanding attention, release. Drinking. Driving.

She had no idea what would have happened if Nathan hadn't been around. He made both of them talk, made them open up to each other until Russ understood that Kelsey needed help.

That was exactly why he would be so furious

when he found out about this, and Dr. Lawrence was right: Her brother would find out. He always did. And he *would* rant and rave, not so much about the protest, but because she hadn't mentioned it, at least not to him.

And why not?

Because she didn't want to hear what he'd have to say? No. She knew what he'd say, and many of the words were those she'd told herself.

So why not?

The answer wasn't clear. She respected Russ and trusted him, and she knew he respected and trusted her. The bond between them was tight, but since their father's death Russ made an issue of everything. If Kelsey forgot to put out the trash, he worried that it somehow had to do with their mother's illness. If she wanted to curl up with a good book rather than go out with friends on Friday night, he asked if she needed grief counseling. Why couldn't he just leave her alone? She was handling life okay. She didn't need a guardian.

Guardian. Kelsey felt her temper begin to swell at the mere thought of that word. She didn't need a keeper. She'd tell him about the protest when it was over. No doubt he'd still lecture her on the value of communication, but at least she wouldn't get grounded. She hated being restricted, a fact Russ knew only too well.

Ratasha asked once why Kelsey let her brother rule. *Let* him rule? As if she had a choice! It wasn't just that he was fourteen years older, but he'd been her mentor, guide, chauffeur, cook, from the time she was born. Their mother's sporadic mental illness added responsibility to her oldest son's life, and he'd matured quickly. Yet his nature was caring, and he had joined in Kelsey's upbringing, not because of duty but because of love. There were times he was annoying, exasperating, and too hotheaded for her taste. But there were also times he praised her, laughed with her, held her when she cried. He, his wife, Amy, and their children, Megan and Charlie, were special. She needed their love and respect, and she knew it.

Even if Russ was sometimes a pain in the—

Someone hissed at her, and she stiffened up. How was she ever going to make another twenty minutes?

Okay, not your hair or your toes. Think about Dan.

A gentle smile spread slowly across Kelsey's face at the thought of Dan Quigley, one of her brothers' best friends. She'd been twelve when he'd walked into her world, a handsome young rookie assigned to partner with Russ, and she'd tumbled head over heels in love. It wasn't Dan's good looks. With her brothers' ever-present friends, she was surrounded by handsome men. And it wasn't his uniform; she was used to that too. But Dan understood her need to expand, to be treated more like the young woman she'd become. While her brothers were still teasing and pestering, Dan brought white roses and stuffed penguins and poems and grins. He listened, and he adjusted to her new moods with the ease of an old shoe. They still kept in touch.

He'd be as upset as Russell if he saw you sitting here, doing nothing.

Kelsey started to sigh but caught the sound in her throat.

Okay, forget Dan. How about some mental calisthenics? Plan your creative writing story due next week. Focus.

Mr. Marshall said he wanted a slice-of-life piece, something emphasizing local color and characterization. Russ's workshop? Her father's office? The protest? Now that would make a good story. She could entitle it "Temporary Insanity."

The bell rang, sounding release, and like a fourth grader ready for summer vacation, Kelsey swiveled her legs to the side. This time the hiss formed into words.

"Follow Drew's lead!"

Drew's lead? He was taking his time, stretching leisurely, whittling away seconds until they turned into minutes while he picked up his notebook, tied his shoestrings, tugged on his socks, and then moseyed out the door. The others followed behind, as if out for a morning stroll, creating chaos and confusion as they spilled into the hall.

Kelsey's heart began to race. Her next class seemed a mile away, down the hall, the stairs, outside—to save time—around the corner.

She almost made it. The bell rang when she was seconds away, and Mr. Marshall duly noted the tardy in his grade book.

Wonderful. Now she had something else to explain to Russell when report cards came out, although one tardy would pale in comparison to her English grade. Mr. Marshall was already teaching, and she hadn't even opened her notebook. She was headachy, out of breath, and wanted to sleep.

It had been one miserable afternoon. Had Drew cast some kind of hypnotic spell over her classmates and absorbed their sanity? Kelsey could still agree with the protest. It was making a physical statement to Mrs. Delaney, but it should have stayed in the classroom, not spilled over into the hall. That had been both insulting and rude.

Well, Kelsey thought, pulling her binder out of her bag, *maybe it is time someone had a talk with Mr. Andrew Jefferson Wilson.*

And maybe that time was soon, like today, after school, before he made plans for tomorrow, plans that would only push life in a direction Kelsey was becoming less and less willing to go.

9

complications

Come on. Come on, Kelsey thought, leaning impatiently against Drew's locker. She just wanted to say what she had to say and get on with it. What was taking so long?

"Thought you had practice."

"I do," Kelsey said, turning toward the speaker with a warm smile. "But I need to talk to Drew."

Terrance put his hand above her head and looked down. "What's up?"

Kelsey shrugged. She wasn't sure herself what she was going to say, so how could she tell Terrance what she didn't know? He raised his eyebrows, waiting.

"What do you think about this whole protest thing?" she asked, changing the subject.

"I think it's wack, man," Terrance said slowly, "but with all the zeros I got, I can't stop now. Not until we work something out."

"You told your mother?" Kelsey asked, craning her neck to look around at an oncoming trio. Still no Drew.

"Naw. You told Big Red?"

Kelsey shook her head. "Guess we're both living on borrowed time."

Still no Drew.

"You want me to give him a message or something?" Terrance asked. "Elliot will have you running bases if you're late."

Kelsey glanced at the hall clock. She still had time to make it if she hurried. "I was going tell him I didn't like his holding up class at the end of the period," she said, leaning over to pick up her athletic bag. "I have to go halfway across the school, to Marshall's class, and it made me late."

"Yeah," Terrance said. "I barely made it to pre-cal, and it's right down the hall."

Kelsey brightened. "Then you'll talk to him?"

"Yeah. I'll see what's up."

"That'd be great!" she said, ducking out from under his long arm. "I owe you one."

"Take the AP exam for me," he said.

"Uh-huh." She shifted the bag to her shoulder. "Like the counselors can't tell us apart."

Terrance laughed and gave her a pat on the head.

"Too bad. I could have used the credit to get more time on the court."

Kelsey smiled as she took off. Terrance was a lot deeper than most people, maybe even he himself, realized. She worked her way through the maze of students, who seemed to come to life after the dismissal bell, and considered the situation. In spite of his long hair and seventies style, Drew liked to be one of the boys. He would probably respond more positively to Terrance than he would have to Kelsey anyway.

She liked Drew. She found him witty and charming and at times a lot of fun, but there was also something about him that made her feel off-balance, as though he'd embarrass her or something if she let her guard down. He was always pushing the teachers, asking questions he didn't think they could answer, talking in a voice too loud for the classroom, not passing a test or paper on down the row, things that messed up routine.

So how did he get put in charge? Kelsey wondered as she entered the tunnel leading to the locker rooms.

Because everyone likes him, she answered herself, shaking her head. He definitely *was* popular, surprisingly so for someone who did not play sports or march with the band. It was as if his quasi-rebellious ways had a magnetic effect that drew people in.

"Sure hope Terrance can talk some sense into him," Kelsey mumbled out loud.

"It's when you start answering yourself that I'm gonna worry."

Kelsey had heard the footsteps coming from behind but hadn't realized her voice would carry down the corridor. She pulled up and waited until Marti came alongside.

"I don't suppose you did your work in English today."

"No," Kelsey answered, pushing the locker room door open with her shoulder.

"Anyone talk to Mrs. Delaney?"

Kelsey shook her head. "Not after Tuesday. When she told us that the way she taught was her business and that our class wasn't a democracy, well, it kind of cut off the desire to communicate. I mean, she was mad, Marti. Really mad."

"Dad still thinks something's up. Delaney's been around the district a long time, and she's always had a good rep."

"I know," Kelsey said. Something had to have changed. Mrs. Delaney was so tired lately, and distant, as if she were existing in her own little world. Maybe she didn't even care that all her students were failing.

"So you gonna talk to Russ tonight?" Marti asked.

"What are you? A reporter?" Kelsey shot back. She felt her face flush and took a deep breath. "It's *my* life."

"Maybe, but you don't live in isolation, Kelsey Gene," Marti replied. "You've got to tell him what's going on."

"Why? So he can throw a fit?" Kelsey asked, dropping down on the center bench in front of her locker. "You know Russ. There are rules. You obey them. If the speed limit is seventy, you don't go seventy-five. Pure and simple. You go to English and do your work." She ran her fingers through her hair. "A protest doesn't fall anywhere within the range of his expectations."

"Then you need to make him understand," Marti said, "make him *feel* your concerns."

Kelsey laughed as she untied her shoelaces. "My big brother? Mr. Trooper in charge of the world? Right. You know Ms. Elliot isn't going to buy an excuse for being late. You'd better go get dressed."

Marti nodded and headed toward her own locker. "You need to talk to him, KG."

"I'll think about it," Kelsey said, standing up.

Think about what? The protest? Russ? Her failing grade in English? She leaned back against the lockers and sighed. She was feeling raggedy, as if she hadn't slept well in days.

Something was going to have to give, and soon, or

all Russ would have to do was look at her and he'd know something was wrong. Then he'd insist that they talk, and when things started out that way, they tended to gather a momentum of their own.

So maybe you should *talk to him*, her conscience urged, and she sighed heavily. How could she argue with herself? She was going to have to tell Russ, and that was all there was to it. But not now, not today.

She'd tell him later, tomorrow, if the protest didn't end.

10

second warning

"HARRIS! BLACKWELL! IN MY OFFICE, NOW!" Ms. Elliot's voice ricocheted off the doors, sounding a thunderous alarm.

Ratasha appeared almost instantly in the aisle off Kelsey's bank of lockers. "What do you wanta bet she's heard?"

Kelsey groaned as she grabbed her glove off the floor. Ms. Elliot kept a constant vigil over her athletes, checking grades and discipline records, asking about family and friends. She felt it was her responsibility as a coach to guide the whole person, not just to develop physical skill, and she worked hard at being true to her convictions. She was intense, sincere, and she didn't like to be let down.

Suzanne Elliot was also one of Amy's closest friends, and while Ms. Elliot made every effort to treat Kelsey like any other student, the coach was as loyal to her friends as she was dedicated to her athletes. If Russ didn't know about the protest yet, no doubt Ms. Elliot would tell him.

"Come on, girl," Ratasha urged. "You know she doesn't like waiting."

Ms. Elliot was leaning against the wall outside her office, hands stuffed deep in her pockets. She nodded toward two waiting chairs, then followed the girls inside, closing the door with a thud.

"Let me tell you a little story," she began, watching the two carefully. "Here I was sitting at lunch, enjoying a salad—lettuce, tomato, a touch of French dressing—when someone said, 'I can't believe your athletes are involved in this, Suzanne. Are you losing your touch?'

"'In what?' I wonder as I take another bite, listening to talk about some protest that apparently two of my seniors have helped start!"

Ms. Elliot's voice had risen, almost overpowering the small room. She paused as she moved around the desk and sat down. "Please tell me that this is all a rumor, or that the lunch conversation was nothing more than a bad practical joke."

Neither girl spoke.

"This is unbelievable! Two months before graduation and you decide to stage a demonstration? Are you insane?"

Kelsey stared at her knees, waiting for the lecture to end.

"Blackwell, does your brother know about this?"

Kelsey shook her head no.

"Harris? Your parents?"

"No, ma'am." At least Ratasha had the strength to talk.

"Well, they are going to find out about it now because I'm calling them!" Ms. Elliot picked up a computer printout from the upper-right corner of her desk, and Kelsey recognized it as the list of emergency contacts. It contained addresses, phone numbers, names of doctors, medical information. The coach ran her finger a third of the way down the page—too far for Blackwell—and picked up the phone.

This was reality. If Russ got the news at work, everything would be worse. Oh, he would act professionally and calmly, the way he always did on duty, but then his anger would turn inward and simmer. Ms. Elliot knew that too, so why was she calling in the middle of the day? What business was it—

"Please." It was Ratasha. "Let me tell them." The words were barely audible.

Ms. Elliot stopped and considered the request. "When?"

"Tonight."

Kelsey held her breath.

"Blackwell?"

She nodded heavily, still voiceless.

The coach dropped the receiver back in the cradle. "I don't know what you two are up to, but you have twenty-four hours to straighten things out or I am going to straighten them out for you." She rose from her desk, crossed behind the girls, and threw open the door. "Go."

The abrupt dismissal caught Kelsey by surprise. She told herself to move and collided with Ratasha in an awkward dance as both tried to squeeze out of the room. The door slammed on their heels.

"I need a minute," Ratasha said, ducking her head to the side. Kelsey saw tears tracking down her friend's cheeks, heard the muffled sobs. Ratasha never cried, not even when she broke her ankle last year sliding into third.

Kelsey turned toward the field, slow-footed, heavy, letting her feet drag through the dry grass. If Elliot knew, then so did Coach Mobly; that ought to make Terrance's day. And Mr. Lazoya had asked JJ to stop by after school. She glanced up and saw Marti waiting a few yards ahead.

"You heard?"

"Who didn't?" Marti asked, falling into step. "She was really upset."

"That she was," Kelsey said wearily.

"So what are you going to do?"

"Tell Russ. Ms. Elliot will call him if I don't, and I can't let him hear this from anyone else."

"No," Marti agreed. "You can't."

Kelsey picked up the pace and worked into a solid jog. Physically a good workout was exactly what she needed. Mentally she wanted to dig a big hole, crawl in, and hide. They were almost to the field before either said anything more.

"I could go with you," Marti offered. "Might help."

Kelsey slowed to a stop. "Only if you waited in the car with the engine running, so I could get away fast."

Marti laughed. "Russ'd love that."

In spite of the dismal prospects, a smile crept across Kelsey's face as she ran the back of her hand across her forehead. Already she was sweating.

She took a ball from her glove and backed up. "I think," she said, sending Marti an easy underhand lob, "that one way or another I've got to find a way out of this mess."

They began a slow exchange, back and forth.

"You can't just end it?" Marti asked after several throws.

"Nope. Not unless Mrs. Delaney agrees to let us make up the work." Kelsey threw a hard toss into Marti's glove. "If she doesn't, we're sunk."

"You could go to the school board," Marti suggested, shooting the ball back. "They probably wouldn't like the fact that the whole AP class is failing."

"But that might hurt her career, and we don't want to do that," Kelsey replied. "Who'd have thought it would go this far?"

Suddenly Ms. Elliot emerged from the locker room with a grim expression, and for the duration of practice her errant seniors had her undivided attention. While others polished fielding skills, Ratasha and Kelsey did push-ups, and sit-ups; ran wind sprints—conditioning, the coach called it—scooped grounders, and practiced sliding, again and again and again. By the time Kelsey finally limped off the field, favoring a sore knee, she was exhausted, irritated, and absolutely convinced she did not want to tell Russ.

As if she had a choice!

She didn't, of course. Ms. Elliot would call tomorrow to check. That was a given, and although Kelsey sometimes ignored her own instincts, she knew better than to push her brother too far. Maybe if Marti did tag along, they could convince Russ that his little sister hadn't gone insane. Maybe he wouldn't worry and fret and fuss and stew. Maybe he'd actually listen, then say, "Okay, Kelsey Gene. Let me know how things turn out."

Right.

Kelsey had about as much of a chance of that happening as she had of growing another head. Like it or not, it was time to face up to the task at hand and tell her brother. Not tomorrow but now. Tonight.

As soon as she got home.

11

spinning around

"Isn't that your car?" Marti asked as they left the gym.

Kelsey frowned at the sight of the familiar blue Renegade parked in the student lot. Nathan was stretched sideways behind the wheel, reading, the top of his dark head resting on the door frame.

"I know my note said you'd drop me off. What's he doing here?"

"Guess there's only one way to find out." Marti shifted her jacket up under her arm and waved.

Nathan yawned lazily and returned the gesture.

"I don't like the feel of this," Kelsey said, watching him squirm around, positioning himself to drive. "Something's up. Maybe something's happened to Russ. Maybe he's been in an accident, or—"

Sudden panic gripped her body, and her feet started to move, taking small staccato steps to build up power to run.

Marti grabbed her arm. "If that were it, he wouldn't be waiting around."

The thought hit them like a twin bolt of lightning. Russ knew! Kelsey whirled around, turning full circle, looking for some escape.

"Gees," she groaned. "He's sent Nathan to get me. What am I going to do?"

"Run?" Marti suggested.

"Think I could beat him?"

"With this head start?" Marti asked. The Jeep was a good fifty yards away. "No way!"

Kelsey laughed in spite of her approaching doom. Although Nathan did not share his siblings' coloring and quick temper, he did have Blackwell tenacity. Like the tortoise and the hare, it wouldn't be his speed but his determination that would win.

"Any last words for a condemned woman?" Kelsey asked as they resumed their stroll.

"If Russ has heard about the protest, KG, he's not going to be happy. It would be a mistake not to take him seriously."

"Meaning?"

"I wouldn't get too righteous with him if I were you," Marti said, stopping at her car. "Even if you are seventeen and he's just your brother."

Kelsey smiled weakly at the effective attack on her

71

favorite complaints. "It'll be hard, but I'll try."

"Call me later?" Marti asked. She opened the door and slid behind the wheel.

"Sure, if I'm alive."

Kelsey stood back, giving Marti room to maneuver out of the parking place and pull away. Was it just this morning that she and JJ had shared coffee? Made their plan? Was it just two days ago that this whole mess had started?

Now what?

Out of the corner of her eye she saw Nathan shift, reminding her he was there, and she turned toward the Jeep. Nothing like a little more excitement for the day. She opened the door and threw her gym bag in the back.

"Judging from the dance you just did, I guess you know why I'm here," Nathan said, waiting for Kelsey to get settled before starting the engine. She pulled her seat belt around while stating the facts.

"Russ wants to see me."

Nathan turned the key. "Care to tell me why?"

The words caught Kelsey by surprise. Although there was a seven-year difference in their ages, her brothers were friends, and like friends, they shared. Nathan usually knew why she was in trouble before she did.

"You really don't know?"

He shook his head. "Russ just called and said he needed to see you."

"So, how'd he sound?" Kelsey asked, staring vacantly out the window at the passing scenery.

"All right. He was at work."

She caught Nathan's questioning glance but didn't turn around. He didn't much like being ignored, but he'd get over it. He was just as apt to fuss as Russ, and she didn't have strength for two rounds.

"That's okay," he said after they'd driven in silence for a long mile. "I can wait."

Kelsey sat up straight. "For what?"

"For Russ to tell me his version."

It was the perfect pitch. Within seconds Kelsey was talking about everything from the first mention of a protest to today.

"So what do you think?" she asked when she finished. Nathan could be a good barometer of their brother's emotional state.

"I think," Nathan said as he turned into their brother's drive, "that Russell is going to see things from a different perspective. He's going to see what the protest might cost, not what it might win."

"So what should I do?" She felt suffocated by a lack of time.

"Listen to him. Answer honestly. Remember he cares."

Kelsey shook her head at the simple words. Talk about direct! "You coming with me?" she asked.

"Nope. I'll be in the house cramming for an exam."

Cramming? Nathan was so organized it was hard to imagine his doing anything at the last minute.

"What? Got a new squeeze?" she asked. He *had* been gone a lot lately.

He grinned at her attempt to pry into his business. "Nothing so nice as that. These last few weekends in the library have eaten away all my free time." He opened the door to get out, and the sound of a sander penetrated the afternoon calm.

"Sounds like he's in the shop, sis," Nathan said, reaching back into the Jeep for his books.

Kelsey fumbled with her seat belt, feeling awkward, confused. Nathan was leaning against the rear fender by the time she finally managed to open the door and crawl out.

"You look like a pup that's about to be drowned," he said, ruffling her hair.

"Oh, Nathan," Kelsey moaned, leaning into his chest. "The sad thing is that Russ and I have been getting along great lately, and this is going to spoil it."

He slipped his fingers under her chin and pulled

her face up. "Not if you listen to him, Kelsey Gene. And not if you make him listen to you." He slid his hand down her back and nudged her forward. "Go on. You know where I'll be if you need me."

Need me? He'd stay if she asked again, but that wouldn't be fair. He wasn't the one who had sat in class for three days protesting his teacher's techniques. He wasn't the one who had hesitated a bit too long to tell Russell what he now already knew. He wasn't the one who had earned this trip to the woodshop for a scolding. No, this was an honor Kelsey had captured all on her own, and it was time to accept that reality by facing Russ.

12

reality check

The door to the shop was open, inviting, warning. Kelsey stopped after only two steps, breathing in deeply, savoring the sweet smell of fresh wood as she imagined her brother's tall form bent over the workbench, sander in hand, forehead wrinkled in concentration. He loved to spend hours alone in the shop, working on his many projects as he worried out problems.

Like the protest? Kelsey wondered.

The sander cut off, leaving a stark silence, and Kelsey's knees locked, freezing her to the ground. If she believed in what they were doing at school, why was it so hard to defend her actions? Why didn't she just square her shoulders, toss her head back, and say, "Hey, big brother. You wanted to see me?"

Perhaps because with each passing hour the line between what was being lost and what she had hoped to gain was becoming more and more blurred.

"Go on now, sis," Nathan said, encouraging her to move. "Russell isn't going to kill you, though he may give you lots of time alone, by yourself, to stare at four walls—"

Kelsey stuck her fingers in her ears, trying not to groan as she slipped quietly through the shop door. There was too much truth in what Nathan said for it to be anything near funny. She settled on the watcher's seat, a high, padded stool positioned to keep spectators out of harm's way.

"Hello, Kelsey Gene."

Russ continued to work, letting the seconds build tension, and Kelsey shot a quick glance toward the open door. If only her legs had enough strength to run. If only she'd told Russ about the protest yesterday, or the day before. If only he'd stop working and—

Abruptly he straightened up, plucked a piece of paper from his pocket, and snapped his wrist to open it up. "Mind explaining this?" he asked, his long arms presenting the sheet within inches of Kelsey's face. It was a form letter advising the "parents/guardian of Kelsey Gene Blackwell" that she was in danger of failing English due to an accumulation of excessive zeros.

She dropped her eyes in silent disbelief and swallowed hard. Progress reports usually went out through the office at specified intervals. Mrs. Delaney had to have sent this one herself.

"Well?" Russ demanded. He leaned back against the workbench and crossed his arms over his chest. "I'm waiting."

"I-I-I know," Kelsey stammered, and finding nothing more suitable to offer, she repeated the phrase.

"If you know so much, please enlighten me."

Kelsey looked up, hunting for an answer. "It's not what you think," she said, but the words stalled, standing in midair, proud and defiant, and she rushed on, trying to cover their sting. "I mean, I am failing, but so's the whole class. We've been protesting by not doing our work."

"The whole class?"

Kelsey nodded. "Mrs. Delaney can't fail all of us, not when she isn't doing her job."

"Mrs. Delaney?" Russ's face still hadn't changed.

Again Kelsey nodded, eager to appear cooperative. "And this is AP English. Most of these kids haven't had a B since kindergarten."

"Mrs. Delaney?" he asked again.

"Uh-huh. You know, fiftyish, slender, smart?"

"She hasn't taught you a thing?"

"What's wrong, Russ? Wearing your earplugs?" She meant the words as a tease, but they came out all wrong.

"My hearing's fine, Kelsey Gene, and you can cut that attitude right now."

"Sorry," she mumbled, sliding off the stool. "But you don't have to be such a grump. I was just kidding."

She walked over to the workbench and picked up a half-finished Victorian frame. "This is pretty. Get a new router?"

"What I got, Kelsey Gene, was a notice in the mail telling me you're failing English." He let the words settle and reestablish focus. Then he went on. "Are we talking about the same Mrs. Delaney who almost drove Nathan crazy?"

Kelsey shrugged. "I guess it's the same one. She's been around forever."

She set the frame down and moved around the bench, then stopped behind her brother. If he needed to play this one out, she wanted to be in a good game position. Russ did a slow pivot and lowered his six-three form to her level, leaning forward on his elbows, destroying her attempt to gain space.

"What makes you think she can't fail the whole class? Seems to me if you refuse to do the work, she has nothing on which to base a grade."

Kelsey tried not to frown. Russ's speech was too precise, too formal, a good indication he was gearing up for one serious lecture. She sidestepped down the length of the table and rounded the corner toward the stool.

"Seems to me if she's refusing to teach, she has nothing to evaluate," she answered.

"I don't understand. If she isn't teaching, what is she grading? Why the zeros?"

Kelsey reached deep for an answer her brother would understand. "This is an AP class, Russ, and all she does is give us papers and papers and more papers. She barely opens her mouth, and to me that's not teaching. So we've decided not to do her busywork."

Russ followed his sister with his eyes. "I see. And that's why you're failing?"

Kelsey nodded.

"Has anyone talked to her?"

"We tried, but she cut us off."

"Did you ask her *why* she'd changed? Maybe she has a reason."

It was a question Kelsey didn't want to answer. "Look, Russ," she said, sliding up onto the seat again, "this isn't as serious as it seems. I just need a little time."

"Time is one thing you don't have, Kelsey Gene. It's almost April. You need senior English to graduate."

Once again he straightened up, assuming what Kelsey called his trooper pose, feet twenty-four inches apart, knees flexed, ready, if necessary, to move, face set in an expressionless mask.

"She's not going to fail the whole class," Kelsey insisted, her anxiety shifting to anger. If Russ wasn't going to listen, why go on?

"And if she does?"

"Then I'll go to summer school."

"Won't that endanger your athletic scholarship?" His questions were coming fast, forcing answers only half formed.

"Maybe the athletic department at the university would approve of someone willing to take a stand," she answered.

"Even if it means missing hockey camp?"

Kelsey frowned.

"You hadn't even thought of that, had you?" Russ asked. "And you expect me to just stand by and watch you throw away your future?"

"You're not listening to me. It won't—"

"Oh, but I am," he interrupted. "And I don't like what I'm hearing. You didn't answer me before. Has anyone bothered asking her—politely—why she's changed? Or have you just gone in and demanded things?"

Kelsey looked away. How could she tell Russ that the protest had started spontaneously, with a will of its own?

"I see. Then maybe all you have to do is meet with her tomorrow and this whole thing will be over."

"You're impossible," she said. She should have known there was no way to have a reasonable discussion with this brother.

"Just to be sure we have communicated," Russ said, "let me make myself perfectly clear. If you don't end this protest, you can stay home this weekend."

"No!" Kelsey shot back. "It's my cause, my future, my life. Marti and I are going—"

"No?" Russ's face reddened in disbelief. "NO?" He lowered himself to within inches of his sister's face. "Either you end the protest tomorrow, Kelsey Gene, or you tell your friends you are unavailable. Understand?"

Kelsey closed her eyes and nodded, not because she'd given in but because it was easier. He straightened back up.

"You wouldn't bully me like this if I were Nathan," she grumbled.

"But you're *not* Nathan, and you're *not* twenty-four, and if you can't figure that out, then this conversation has deteriorated beyond all hope." He offered his sister his hand, and she used it to balance while she slid off the stool. "You going to end this protest?"

"I'll talk to the others," she said.

Russ shook his head, accepting the words for what they were, an offer to try with no promise of success. He motioned Kelsey to go outside, then followed her through the door. "Wait in the car. I'll send Nathan out."

"That's it?" she asked, staring at her brother's back as he passed her by. Maybe he'd forgotten.

"Yep."

"Russell?"

Without missing a step, he stuffed his hands in his pockets, and casually, deliberately walked farther and farther away.

"Ruuusss!"

"Stop by after school tomorrow if the protest doesn't end," he called over his shoulder, and he disappeared into the house.

Kelsey gaped at the empty doorway. Always before when they'd fussed, he'd ended the argument in the Blackwell tradition, with a hug. And in spite of whatever clash they'd had, in spite of whatever medicine Russ had dished out, Kelsey had still felt cherished.

So why was this time different? What was he saying?

Kelsey stood in the middle of the driveway, alone, and wrapped her arms around herself, trying not to cry, trying not to acknowledge the fact that she was being forced to make a choice: obey her brother or stand with her friends. How could Russ do this? Why couldn't he understand that things were not always that simple? Slowly she rocked back and forth, overwhelmed with hopeless frustration, hugging herself tighter, tighter, willing herself not to think until finally, reluctantly the tears began to flow.

One way or another she was going to have to make some kind of sense out of her life. One way or another she was going to have to make her brother understand.

13

morning reflections

All JJ had said before he hung up was "Meet at Mickey D's," and for once Kelsey was first. She sat in a corner booth, slumped down, sipping her coffee while she watched him cruise through the lot, deftly weaving his Mustang around the cleanup crew hosing down the pavement. It took several minutes for him to order his morning fix of Dr Pepper and Egg McMuffin. Obviously JJ's father had taken the failure notice better than Russ.

He set his tray on the table before slouching down in the seat opposite Kelsey and turned to gaze out the window. "The only good news I have on this beautiful day is that my parents haven't seen this." He reached into an inside pocket and pulled out an envelope. It was addressed to "the parents/guardian of Javier Juarez."

"I owe Terrance one," he admitted.

"Terrance?" Kelsey asked, reading a failure report like her own.

"He checked the mail, found his letter, and called me. I tried to catch you, but you weren't home."

Kelsey took a deep swallow of coffee and nodded toward the tray. "Your breakfast is getting cold."

JJ frowned as he undid the wrapping. "Hey, I've known you since kindergarten." He nibbled a piece of egg hanging over the edge of the muffin. "What's up?"

He took a bigger bite of his sandwich, then brought his eyes up to meet Kelsey's. She looked away, trying to formulate a half-truth to cover her worry, but this was JJ, and he *was* a friend.

"Russ is my guardian, remember?" she said. "Mail from the school goes to him."

"Oh, no," JJ groaned, "not Big Red! That's why you didn't answer your phone."

Kelsey nodded. "I had been granted the privilege of a private audience with His Highness to discuss my shortcomings."

"And what was his royal decree?" JJ asked.

"I'm grounded for the weekend unless I quit protesting."

JJ shook his head slowly. "This is really getting serious."

"You're telling me! Marti and I have been planning

to go to this softball tournament for a month, and Russell isn't going to waver."

They sat in silence while JJ finished his sandwich, slowly, again staring out the window at what he had called a beautiful day, but his face no longer glowed.

"I'll take your side if you want to ask the others to quit."

"Have you decided we're wrong?" Kelsey asked.

"No," he answered, looking sad. "But I don't think we're going to win. It would have killed my mother to open this." He reached out for the envelope and stuffed it back into his pocket. "Maybe we got into this thing too fast."

"That's what Russ thinks too. He wants me to talk to Mrs. Delaney, find out what's up."

JJ's face grew serious as he considered the comment. "Are you going to do it?"

"I want to talk to the others first. Maybe we could all hang around together after class or stop by after school or something."

JJ nodded toward the parking lot. "I bet they'll agree. The failure notices scared them."

Kelsey glanced outside in time to see Terrance unfolding from Ratasha's Ford Escort.

"I don't see where he stashes those legs." Kelsey laughed as first one limb, then the other emerged from behind the door. "Bet he'll accept a ride on to school if you offer."

JJ sucked the last of his Dr Pepper up the straw and grinned. "Bet he'd even buy me another drink."

"Probably," Kelsey said, and she lowered her voice. "Listen, JJ, don't tell Marti what Russ said. Nathan has a research project due, so he'll be at the library all weekend. I think I can sneak out."

JJ cocked an eyebrow. "I would think Marti would be easier to soothe than Big Red."

She sighed. JJ was right. Marti would be the easier of the two to handle. But who was she kidding? Russ would find out. He always did, and he'd be furious and make her life miserable. Kelsey shot JJ a quick glance and mouthed a four-letter word.

"Nicely unsaid," he whispered as he swiveled to make room for Ratasha.

"Terrance will be here in a minute," she said, scooting in. She laid her cheek against JJ's shoulder. "Thanks for the warning last night."

"A pleasure."

Ratasha lifted her head, took one look across the table, and poured half of her sixteen-ounce coffee into Kelsey's empty cup. "You okay, girl? You tell your brother?"

Kelsey shrugged, staring at her hands. Why go into it all?

"She wasn't as lucky as we were," JJ said quietly. Kelsey glanced up, glaring, but he was ready for the attack. "They need to know, Kelsey Gene."

"What?" Ratasha asked, her eyes traveling back and forth between the two.

Kelsey recognized defeat. "The letter went to Russ. He thinks maybe we should talk to Mrs. Delaney, ask her what's up."

"Who's Russ?" Terrance asked, setting his tray down at the next table. One by one he removed his juice, milk, scrambled egg breakfast, and extra hash browns, then leaned toward JJ, waiting for an answer.

"You know, Big Red."

"Oh, yeah," Terrance said.

"The point is, we haven't really asked her what's up, why this semester's different."

"Why should we?" Terrance inserted, wolfing down his food. "She's the one not doing her job."

"And we're the ones not doing ours," JJ said. "Maybe it *is* time we talked."

Kelsey frowned. A split decision wasn't going to work.

"Listen, Terrance," she said, "Ms. Elliot is one of the best coaches I know. In the three years I've played for her she's pushed me, praised me, and at times made me want to shove back, but she's always tried, always cared. Wouldn't you agree, Ratasha?"

Kelsey looked across the table and waited for a nod.

"Now say next year Elliot stopped coaching, just sat on the sidelines and watched. Something wouldn't be right."

Kelsey had his attention. "First semester Mrs. Delaney taught the way Ms. Elliot coaches."

She'd picked the right comparison. If there was one thing Terrance understood, it was the discipline of sports. "You saying Mrs. Delaney may have a reason?"

"We won't know if we don't ask. I certainly have nothing to lose. Russ got the letter."

"You know, it's only a matter of time until our parents find out. We were lucky yesterday." The voice was Ratasha's, quiet, strong, rational.

"I guess it wouldn't hurt to ask around, see how the rest of the class feels," Terrance said.

"I vote we talk to Mrs. Delaney," JJ said, and the others nodded. "Like now, before school."

"That way we could pass the word if we reach some sort of compromise," Terrance put in.

"What about Drew?" Kelsey asked, wondering how they would deal with his charisma. "You talk to him yesterday?"

"Yeah," Terrance said, pulling the word out into one long syllable. "We kind of got into it."

"Is that what you two were fussing about? The protest?" JJ asked.

"Yeah."

"You should have seen it. One minute they were standing around talking, and the next they're yelling at each other. Teachers poured out of their rooms as if they thought there was going to be a big fight or something."

"Why?" Ratasha asked.

Terrance shrugged. "He was acting so uppity, you know, like he was the only one who had a brain. I just wanted to bring him down a little."

Ratasha rolled her eyes. "Did any of the teachers write you up?"

"Didn't have to," JJ said, a bit more somber. "Mr. Arnold was walking right by. He saw everything. Made Drew go with him right then and told Terrance to stop by first thing this morning."

"Wonderful," Kelsey mumbled.

"He knows I stay out of trouble," Terrance said, raising his eyebrows mischievously. "And he likes my outside shot."

Kelsey grinned in spite of the serious conversation.

"So Drew's going to be a problem," JJ observed.

"Why?" Ratasha came back. "If the others still want to follow along, fine, but *no* one can make me sit in class and do nothing but me."

Heads nodded, and inwardly Kelsey sighed in relief. She might not have a majority, but at least she wasn't alone. And if Ratasha, Terrance, and JJ were ready to bend, maybe others were too. Maybe she'd be racing over to Russ's after school to tell him this whole mess was over. She'd still have to listen to a lecture—he would never let her off without saying a few words—but that was okay because then he'd hug her and send her home and she could go to the tournament with Marti.

And finally life would be back on track.

14

a simple request

"What's up?" Marti asked as she rounded the corner to the dressing room.

Kelsey was lying on a center bench, eyes closed. "Ms. Elliot here yet?" She stretched her arms over her head and arched her stiff back. "I need to talk to her."

"Her car's here, but I didn't see a light on in her office."

Kelsey sighed. All the hope and anticipation that had been with her when she left McDonald's had quickly vanished with the news that Mrs. Delaney was out for the day.

"You talk to Nathan?" Marti asked, getting her books out of her locker.

"Some. He stopped by my room after you called and asked if I was okay. We talked for a while, but then he started asking me questions about Dad and stuff, and I didn't want to go there."

"Why?"

"Whenever something happens, both he and Russ act like I'm messed up because Dad died. Well, the protest has nothing to do with that." Kelsey swung her legs over the bench and sat up. "So I told him I was tired and wanted to go to bed."

"Nathan's pretty good at helping you with the emotional stuff, KG," Marti said, shuffling through a pile of books. "Maybe you shouldn't blow him off."

"You too?" Kelsey asked. "This has nothing to do with my father!" Her voice echoed through the empty locker room, testifying loudly to her frustration. "Don't say a word," she told Marti. "Besides, you know you don't blow off Nathan Blackwell. He said we'd talk about it later, and he won't forget."

The sound of footsteps shuffling down the hall closed the conversation.

"Sounds like Elliot's here," Kelsey said, getting up.

"You need me to go with you?" Marti asked, still trying to sort through her locker.

Kelsey shouldered her bag. "Thanks, but I've got this one. See you at lunch."

She left the locker room glad that Marti hadn't insisted on more. What she was going to say, what she was about to do, didn't need an audience.

"May I talk to you a minute?" Kelsey asked after rapping lightly on the office door.

Ms. Elliot was sitting behind her desk, holding a mug of steaming coffee between both hands. "Sure. Have a seat." She kicked out the chair beside the desk and leaned back while Kelsey settled in. "You tell your brother about the protest?"

"He knows." Kelsey said, "But that's not why I'm here. I need you to do something for me."

Ms. Elliot put down her coffee and leaned forward on her elbows. Never before had Kelsey made such a bold request of any teacher.

"We'd decided to talk to Mrs. Delaney today," she said, retreating a little, surprised by her own daring. "But she's not here."

Ms. Elliot nodded. "I saw her name on the sub list. No one seems to know why she's out."

"And we can't end the protest until we talk to her."

"Sure you can," Ms. Elliot said, reaching for her mug. "Go in there, do your work, and talk to Mrs. Delaney on Monday."

Kelsey shook her head. "We can't. Not until Mrs. Delaney agrees to let us make up the zeros. If she doesn't, we'll still fail."

"Are you sure?"

"Yes. We all figured our averages, and there is no way we can pull out of this unless Mrs. Delaney will compromise."

The coach took a long sip, then leaned back in her

chair. "So what do you need from me?"

"I need you to get the work off the table and give it to me."

Ms. Elliot raised her eyebrows. "And just how do you propose I do that?"

"You have a master key. All coaches do."

The look of mild surprise that had settled on the coach's face deepened into total disbelief. "And you want me to use it to take something from another teacher's room?"

Kelsey shrugged. "I guess that's what I'm asking. JJ tried following the janitor in yesterday, but—"

"No way, Kelsey Gene," Ms. Elliot interrupted. "It goes against everything I believe in."

Kelsey scooted to the end of the chair. "Okay. I had to ask."

"Wait a minute," Ms. Elliot said. "Why do you want these packets?"

Kelsey settled back. The coach seemed to be listening. "I want to be able to show Mrs. Delaney that this protest hasn't been about doing the work, but rather about her methods. I want to do the assignments to show I still want to learn."

"I see. And when do you plan to talk to her?"

"As soon as she comes back to school."

Ms. Elliot leaned back in her chair and cradled her

forehead in her right hand. She had a habit of thinking things through carefully before making any comment. It seemed forever before she raised her head and squinted, an expression Kelsey knew only too well meant that she'd reached a decision.

"I'll talk to the sub and see what I can work out."

"Thanks," Kelsey said, again scooting forward.

"But—"

Why does there always have to be a "but"? Kelsey asked herself, tensing.

"As soon as Mrs. Delaney is back, I'm telling her what I've done, and if she has *any* objection—"

"There won't be," Kelsey said, cutting the coach off. "I'll explain everything when I talk to her."

Ms. Elliot nodded. "Anything else?"

"No, ma'am," Kelsey said, getting up, "except that I appreciate this."

The coach gave a nod of dismissal, and Kelsey wasted no time leaving. The conversation had gone as well as could be expected, and there was no use lingering, saying too much. The day was not exactly going according to plan, but at least something was being done. If Ms. Elliot could get one packet, copies could be made and distributed to the others. Then, when they talked to Mrs. Delaney and could show her that they were not against working, maybe she'd understand and really start teaching again.

Just like maybe Russ will understand that the protest didn't end?

That was not a thought Kelsey wanted to stay with long. She'd considered calling him the minute she heard Mrs. Delaney was going to be out, but the only thing he wanted to hear was that she'd done her work. And she couldn't tell him that—at least not yet.

His words rattled around in her brain: *Stop by after school tomorrow if the protest doesn't end.*

Why? she wondered. What was he going to do?

You'll find out soon enough, she told herself, *so stop worrying about it.*

Right. As if she could turn off her impending doom like a faucet. Without a doubt, this was going to be one very long day, and all Kelsey could do was wait it out—one second at a time.

15

price of glory

When the shop was dark, the first place Kelsey would look for Russ was the backyard, and she found him there, reclining on a chaise lounge, watching the evening sky change colors. He scrunched his legs slightly toward the edge, inviting her to join him.

"You want the good news or the bad news first?" she asked, reluctantly accepting the offered space. She would have preferred more distance, like a few thousand miles of telephone line, but options were nil.

"Always start with the good," he said, watching while she got settled. "It softens the blow."

"Okay. I talked to some of the others this morning, and we agreed we need to talk to Mrs. Delaney."

"And the bad news?"

"She was absent today."

"Did she leave an assignment with the sub?"

Kelsey considered a lie, but she hated deceit.

"Actually she left a test," she admitted.

"And did you do it?"

She felt his eyes lock onto the side of her face. "No. We wanted to talk to Mrs. Delaney before, you know, we—"

"What? Quit? Gave in? Is it just a matter of pride?"

Kelsey wilted. "I don't know anymore, Russ. It's as if the protest has a will of its own."

For a brief second she thought he was going to squeeze her shoulder, a family sign of support, but he stopped as if catching himself and folded his hands behind his neck.

"What was the reaction to yesterday's mail?" To Kelsey's relief, his voice no longer carried an angry edge.

She smiled weakly. "Actually you're the only one who fussed."

"I can't believe Terrance's mother appreciated a failure notice, or JJ's dad," Russ said with surprise. "They take a big interest in their kids, and—"Awareness quickly dawned. "They didn't get them, did they?"

Kelsey leaned toward her brother. "That should be one thing in my favor, right?"

"Wrong," he said. "The only reason you got caught was that I happened to get the mail. Why didn't you talk to me when this thing first happened?"

"Because I'm old enough to make decisions on my own, Russ," she said.

"Not on something like this."

She gave up. She should have followed her initial instincts and talked to Russ at the 7-Eleven. But she hadn't, and now she was in one heck of a jam.

"So am I grounded?" she asked, instead of answering his question.

Russ raised his eyebrows. "Did you end the protest?"

"No, but we talked about it and—"

"By not taking the test, you're actually in worse shape than you were yesterday, right?"

Kelsey shrugged.

"Then yes, you're grounded for the weekend. You know the routine."

"That's an understatement," Kelsey said, standing up. She waited for Russ to move, but his gaze stayed fixed on the horizon.

She decided to give it one last shot. "You know, this isn't fair to Marti. She didn't do anything wrong."

Russ's eyes shifted to his sister. "You knew what would happen when you sat in class today doing nothing."

"But we're ready to end the protest. We just haven't had the chance to talk to Mrs. Delaney yet."

"Enough, Kelsey Gene," Russ said, returning to the sky. "Go on home now, and check your computer. There's a message waiting."

Dismissed again? Thrown out like yesterday's trash?

Who gave Russ the right to interfere in her life? Their dad's will said "guardian," not coldhearted dictator. What had gotten into him?

She rocked back on her heels and spun away before she said more than she should, something that would really rile her stubborn brother. It was like he'd stepped back emotionally ten paces and he was treating her with the same detachment he'd display to a motorist he'd caught speeding. *May I please see your license and proof of insurance, ma'am? Did you know you were going seventy-two, ma'am? I'm going to have to write you a ticket, ma'am.*

By the time Kelsey arrived home she was tempted to turn around, go back, and make Russ fight it out. Somehow, though, he hadn't seemed in the mood to quarrel. She headed straight upstairs, threw her gym bag on the floor, and then stared at her computer for a good five minutes before finally booting up. A message appeared instantly:

> As part of your restriction, you are to send one message every half hour you are not sleeping, as well as at other times I designate. Do you understand?

"In your dreams, Russell," she muttered, flipping off the hard drive. No way could he make her check in like some criminal wearing an ankle restraint. No way was she going to let him badger her like—

The soft jingle of the phone rattled against Kelsey's nerves, and she fumbled for the receiver.

"Hello?"

"The first check-in time is seven forty-three."

"And if I don't?" she yelled into the mouthpiece, but the line was already dead.

Kelsey's mouth fell open. Russ had hung up on her! Who did he think he was anyway? Furiously she punched in the numbers to call him back, but sanity surfaced before she connected, and she put the receiver down.

Maybe there was a better way to play this game. She settled in, pulled up the initial menu, and clicked on the control panel, hunting the clock, while she wondered how difficult it would be to create a program that would send messages through the modem at later, designated times.

A request for a password flashed onto the center of the screen. Password? She'd never needed a password before. Quickly she checked other icons. The ones where she stored her games were also blocked. Only Microsoft Word and Chase, which she'd used to pay the household bills since her mother's hospitalization, were open. Even AOL now had child restraints.

"What do you expect me to do, Russell!" Kelsey said, slamming her desk with her open palm. "Turn my back on my friends?"

She threw herself onto the bed and grabbed a pillow out from under her spread.

That's probably exactly what he expects, she thought, burying her face in the softness. How many times had they talked about the importance of independence, of listening to your own heart? She hated when Russ fussed at her, but Mrs. Delaney was wrong, and she was going to stick with her friends. He'd just have to get over it. He was her brother, not her father, so why was he treating her like this?

Last time he'd grounded her he made her stay at his house, in the guest room. She'd read a wonderful book, enjoyed Amy's home cooking, and it was hardly like punishment at all—except that she'd missed one of the best parties of the year.

So why the computer? What was he doing? Was it a conscious effort to wear her down, make her give in?

If so, it was working, because even though she tried to pretend it didn't matter, it did. She missed him. She missed Amy and the kids. She missed hanging out after practice, laughing, eating, watching TV. She missed her family.

No doubt about it. She was going to have to find a way out of this mess, and soon, before Russ's new-found attitude settled in like a bad habit, chipping away at all she held dear.

16

solitary confinement

Russ followed their father's rules for confinements: no phone, TV, music, computer games, or leaving your room except to eat. Grounding wasn't meant to be pleasant, and even though no one was home to supervise, Kelsey knew two things: Russ's computer surveillance would make it impossible to sneak out, and by Sunday she'd be miserable.

Calling Marti only made things worse. It wasn't just any tournament they'd planned to attend, but one where they could scope out the level of play Kelsey would face in college. It wasn't easy for her to offer up her tickets or listen to Marti's disappointment.

At seven-thirty she booted up the computer and played around, trying to find something she'd missed during her first rushed effort, like a way to bypass the new security codes. Nothing surfaced. She couldn't even load new programs, though with all the homework, that was probably a blessing. Now she would be forced to concentrate on school, with no tempting distractions from video games.

She glanced at the clock, logged on to AOL, and sent Russ an E-mail:

It's 7:42.

Seconds later an instant message flashed back:

Did you call anyone?

Kelsey's mouth dropped open. He was questioning her honesty?

That hurts, Russell!

Answer the question, Kelsey Gene.

Her fingers flew across the keyboard, pounding in defiance.

I called Marti. Okay? I had to tell her I
can't go tomorrow!

OK. Send the next message at 8, and every

half hour afterward until you go to bed
unless otherwise instructed.

Do you want me to embroider a scarlet G on
my chest, too? For grounded?

Russ disconnected. So much for dialogue. Kelsey used the time between contacts to down a quick bowl of soup. She felt hungry, but her stomach was too tight for anything heavy. It took until nine-thirty, when she again saw him on-line, for her to feel settled enough to question her brother's motives.

It's 9:30, Russell, and I want to talk to you!

I'm listening, Kelsey Gene.

Why are you doing this?

Your next check in time is 10:02.

Russell!!!

Again Russ signed off. Kelsey thought about phoning, but she didn't want to hear him hang up. Okay, if this was the way he wanted it, she could accept his terms. She showered, thumbed through a magazine, and started a load of laundry before the next deadline. When she signed on and glanced at her buddy list, Russ was already on-line.

It's 10:02. Why you won't you answer my question?

Because you already know the answer, Kelsey Gene.

If I promise not to sneak out, will you stop this silly surveillance?

No. Check in again at 10:25.

No? Had she lost his trust too? Shattered, Kelsey lowered her face into her hands and cried, unleashing the pressure that had built up for hours. Days of anger and frustration mingled into a hot bitter flow until she was exhausted and dry. At the next scheduled link she felt mildly grateful for the electronic wall Russ had forced between them. No way did she want him to see her red, puffy eyes.

It's 10:25, Russell. I'm going to bed.

Sleep tight.

Kelsey spent most of the night tossing and turning. At six she gave up and rose, out of sorts, wondering what to do with the rest of her day. Clean closets? Count earrings? Write notes? Swell. That should take her to noon.

One second at a time. Don't think of more.

Downstairs she fixed a pot of coffee, grabbed the largest mug she could find—a Saturday cup, as Nathan called it—and filled it two-thirds of the way full before heading back to her room. Russ knew she was an early riser. If she didn't check in soon, he'd be on his way over, and the way she felt, meeting face-to-face would be like putting a match to dynamite and watching it blow.

She set the cup to the right of the keyboard and logged on. Russ liked to spend his Saturday mornings checking his investments and writing friends as he eased into his day. As she'd expected, he was already on-line.

```
Good morning, Kelsey Gene. Please record
the time you wake up.


Noon.


Try again.
```

Kelsey smiled. It was definitely her elder brother on the other end.

```
It's 6:45. Have you had your second cup of
coffee?
```

```
Yes.
```

```
Then will you answer one question?
```

She held her breath. While she didn't want to see Russ, she did need to feel a part of his life.

```
Perhaps.
```

Good. He didn't say no.

```
What would you have done if you'd been in
my shoes?
```

```
When I was in school we did what our teach-
ers asked or our coaches took care of the
situation. I can't believe Suzanne is pleased
about this.
```

```
She isn't.
```

```
Then maybe you should try listening to her.

Please check in each half hour.
```

No! Kelsey thought. *Not yet!*

```
Wait! I'm not through!
```

```
I am.
```

Russ signed off, and the rest of the day churned along at an agonizing pace. Nathan stumbled through to bed about four with barely a hello, leaving his sister to fill the long hours alone. She pieced together a jigsaw puzzle, did schoolwork, and wrote in her journal until the drivel stopped making sense even as a means of moving time. Every half hour she dutifully checked in, only to be met by a blank screen. It wasn't until dinnertime, when she should have been out with Marti, that Russ came back on-line with questions, personal questions only Kelsey could answer.

```
What was Dad's favorite color?
```

```
Blue.
```

```
What was the name of the turtle you had
```

in seventh grade?

"He's making sure it's me!" Kelsey declared to the walls. "I'm not believing this."

Humpty, and it was fifth grade.

Another question flashed immediately.

What is Charlie's middle name?

Ward.

How can you tell when potatoes are done?

They float to the top!

It was an old family joke, utter nonsense, but a way they used to tell someone to butt out.

So did I pass?

Your next check-in is at 8:48.

Russ signed off before Kelsey could respond, and by the next check she was ready to fight.

It's 8:48. I see you're on-line.

When was the last time you visited Mom?

Three Saturdays ago. When was the last time
you did?

Today. When is Megan's birthday?

April 24th, and Charlie's is March 12th.
Why are you acting so distant? Why can't you
see my side?

Distance gives me perspective.

Perspective for what?

Check in again at 9:07.

He was giving her less and less time between
check-ins, undoubtedly to be sure she stuck around.
Kelsey found herself watching the clock almost
eagerly, focusing on the next contact. Again, Russ was
already connected.

It's 9:07.

Why has it been so long since you visited
Mom?

I haven't felt like it. Why is it so important to you that I end this protest?

Because this has real possibilities of growing
into something much more serious. What did you
give Dad for his fiftieth birthday?

An essay.

Please elaborate.

Kelsey's fingers froze. That wasn't an idle question. Russ knew how hard it was for her to talk about
their dad. He was interrogating her, carefully and con-
sciously digging deeper into motives, asking if somehow the protest had anything to do with their father's
death or their mother's dementia. She answered
quickly and accurately, hoping to mollify his concerns
before they mushroomed.

An essay I wrote on fatherhood. He kept it
in a scrapbook of memories on the shelf
behind his desk.

115

Kelsey's breath hung in her throat. It was a fine line between saying too much and too little. Either would send up a red flag, and Russ would have her talking to a shrink, and then Nathan would get involved, and—

Are you alone?

Good, Kelsey thought, exhaling in relief.

You know it's against the rules to have anyone over when I'm grounded.

Answer the question.

Yes. I'm alone. How could you ask such a thing?

Because I know you, Kelsey Gene. Check in again at 9:30.

She shook her head, wondering if he had any inkling of the irony of her answer. It wasn't that she was being compliant. When she was grounded, her casual friends were too scared of Russ to come over, and her close ones too respectful. Still, he'd asked the question, testing her, letting her know he wasn't a fool.

As if she could ever mistake him for one! She made the next contact brief, even though Russ was logged on.

It's 9:30, and I'm going to bed.

She exited the program without waiting for a response, and the phone rang within thirty seconds.

"Hello, Russell," she answered, laughing at his predictability. He was definitely the same old brother.

"Good night, Kelsey Gene."

The click was immediate. So much for the human touch. Russ didn't connect again until late Sunday night, but surprisingly the day went well. Kelsey found a new novel sitting on the coffeepot when she went down for breakfast, undoubtedly put there by Nathan when he left before dawn. It was a new Dean Koontz, and the writing was fast-paced and vivid. She read slowly, savoring every word. If she knew Nathan, next week he'd make a comment or ask a question that would lead into a lively discussion of the book. It was his way of caring, though sometimes she suspected his need to listen was as keen as hers was to talk.

In between chapters she worked on an assignment for creative writing, the first draft of the short story due on Wednesday. Mr. Marshall always told his students to write about what they knew, that their writing would be more passionate if the words came from the heart. Kelsey chose a memory of the day Russ's son, Charlie, had been born. She saw herself standing outside the nursery window watching him looking around with wonder, and she'd tried to imagine what he saw. Lights? Glass? Giants? She wondered if he had any perspective, if he knew he was a little guy. In the end, the piece was more a personal essay than a short story, but the effort had taken several hours, and she ended up with something to save and perhaps someday share with her nephew.

Between the story and the novel, the day eased on. It wasn't until the eight-thirty check-in that Russ again came on-line.

```
It's 8:30 and all is well.
```

It was the standard statement she'd used for more than twelve hours, only this time a message came back.

```
You've been very accurate with your time
today.
```

Kelsey couldn't believe it. Words! She typed quickly.

```
What? A compliment? I must be dead!
```

```
Not funny. Good-bye.
```

Russ was definitely on the other end. Her smart-mouth remarks grated against his patience almost as much as her cussing did.

```
Don't go. Please?
```

It was almost a minute before a message came back.

```
Okay.
```

Good. She'd been waiting all day for a chance to get him talking.

```
You evaded my question yesterday.
```

```
What question?
```

Innocence, the same ploy she'd use.

```
The one about what you would do if you were
in my shoes.
```

```
I'd think about the difficult decision I
was forcing on my older brother.
```

What do you mean?

If you do not end your involvement in this
protest, you are forcing me to end it for you.

The words struck a nerve that had been aching all
weekend.

Why? It's my life!

I owe it to Dad.

It was exactly what she thought.

Damn it, Russell, I'm tired of hearing you
say that. If Dad were here, he'd understand.

Would he? Because if you think our father
would have approved of this inane mess at
school, Kelsey Gene, we were raised by two
different people.

Russ was gone.

A wave of melancholy fluttered around and landed
hard on Kelsey's heart. As usual, he was right. Their dad

had no tolerance—none—for misbehaving at school. If he'd been alive she probably would have talked to him after class Tuesday, listened to his advice, and then acted accordingly even if it had meant standing alone.

So why did she get so furious with Russ? Why did she struggle so hard to be independent when she knew she wanted both brothers in her life?

Once, when Kelsey was complaining about Russ's interference, Nathan asked her to imagine what she would do if she found herself suddenly responsible for Megan. Unlike Charlie, who seemed born with common sense, Megan was redheaded, fiery, and absolutely convinced she could do everything. It wasn't that she was a bad child. She openly loved her parents and tried to please, but she was full of curiosity and intelligence and questions that tempted her beyond a two-year-old's skill. Russ and Amy worked hard at teaching their daughter to act in an acceptable way, and their efforts were being rewarded. Megan was emerging from the terrible twos into a pleasant, well-behaved preschooler. If something happened to Amy and Russ, Kelsey *knew* she would try to pattern their example in bringing Megan up.

The way Russ was patterning their dad's?

Nathan had made his point, which Kelsey noticed was still hanging around. Her brother was doing only what their dad had asked him to do in his will, which wasn't much different from what Russ had done most of his life. He'd always helped take care of her, but without their father as a buffer, someone to whom she could appeal, it just plain felt wrong.

Kelsey wanted Russ to be a brother; she wanted her father to be alive. But that wasn't going to happen. Things changed, and she needed to adjust. She knew Russ was only trying to do what he thought was best. Maybe it was time she tried to see *his* side of things more.

Maybe it was time she gave him a break.

17

day five

Kelsey sat, hands folded neatly on top of her empty desk, back straight, eyes focused on the board directly ahead. It was routine now, a dull, tedious routine. Thank heaven it was the last time. She was determined to do something besides wait for another day, even though her teacher was absent again. Talking at lunch—quietly, among themselves—Kelsey, Ratasha, JJ, and Terrance resolved to go by Mrs. Delaney's house after practice. She'd always been reasonable—that is, before last week. Surely if they shared their concerns *and* asked about hers, an agreement could be reached. They would do the makeup work, and she would start teaching again. It was that simple. All it would take would be an honest exchange.

So, Kelsey wondered, *why do I feel like I've swallowed a handful of pins and they're moving down my throat, into my veins, into my brain, driving me insane?*

She jumped as someone's fingers wrapped around both her upper arms and dug into her flesh.

"Blackwell, either you walk out of here, or so help me, I will drag you." The voice was Ms. Elliot's, who apparently had come in through the back door. "Do you understand?"

There was no hesitation in Kelsey's nod. She felt the grip tighten even more as the coach pulled, bringing Kelsey to her feet, out of her seat, into the aisle, as if she were someone else. Only she wasn't. She was Kelsey Gene Blackwell, and she knew without question that if she stumbled, her coach wouldn't stop. Mr. Lazoya barreled through the door as they were leaving, seconds before Ms. Elliot backed Kelsey into the bank of lockers lining the wall.

"Move so much as an inch, and I will personally deliver you to Russ."

The coach disappeared into the classroom and emerged in less than a minute, towing a gray-faced Ratasha behind.

"Come on," she growled, catching Kelsey's arm and hauling her on one side, Ratasha on the other, down the hall. "I told you to stop this nonsense, but did you listen? No! You had to keep pushing, on and on, pushing and pushing, till you forced the administration to take action."

She turned the corner and headed to the stairs. "I hope Russell grounds you until you're an old woman, Blackwell, locks you up and throws away the key, or, better yet, makes you move in with him. And Harris, if you thought telling your parents about the protest was hard, wait till you hear this."

Together they bumped down the steps in giant leaps, hitting the floor with a thud. Ms. Elliot stopped, and Kelsey and Ratasha flew on by, jerking to a halt when they reached the end of the coach's arms. She waited until the girls turned around before delivering her news.

"You're being suspended. Do you realize that?"

The words collided against Kelsey's ear with a painful sting, and her breath stopped.

"Aha," Elliot said, nodding slowly as her eyes jumped from one face to the other. "I see reality has finally taken hold."

A tiny squeak escaped from Kelsey's throat as her lungs cried out, desperate for air, and she gasped.

"Why?" Ratasha asked, her voice childlike, small.

The coach released her hold and let her arms fall. "There is quite a fuss going on." She sounded more tired than mad. "Parents have been calling; the administration is upset. Then there was that ruckus between Terrance and Drew after school Thursday." Ms. Elliot stopped to gather her thoughts. "The thing is, ladies, they've interviewed some of the kids, and they are saying that you two, Terrance, Drew, and JJ started the whole thing."

Kelsey's body jerked in reaction. "We started it? WE started it?" She spun around. "*We* are the ones trying to figure a way out. We're—"

"Settle down," the coach said in her no-nonsense, do-it-now voice.

Kelsey slapped her forehead with her open palm. When was it ever going to end?

"That's better," Ms. Elliot said. "Having a temper fit here in the hall isn't going to help a bit. It may very well be that you had nothing to do with starting this thing, but we can deal with that later. Now we are going to the office."

"But," Ratasha cut in, her voice still thin, "can they do that? Suspend only a few of us? The whole class participated."

Ms. Elliot's lips curled into an ironic smile. "Oh, they can do anything they want. If it isn't exactly legal, they'll clean it up later." She shook her head. "Look, reality is that they are bluffing here a little, probably hoping that by making an example of you five, the others will get scared and start doing their work."

Kelsey threw her head back and closed her eyes,

repeating the phrase that was becoming an old song. "We've got to get Mrs. Delaney to let us make up the work, or we'll all fail. We have too many zeros. The others know that. They can't stop now."

"And what would you say if you did meet with Mrs. Delaney?" Mrs. Elliot's words had an angry edge. "We're sorry we embarrassed you? Made you look silly in front of your colleagues? Didn't bother to tell you—"

"Drew tried!" Kelsey protested. "And even Ratasha told her we just wanted her to teach, like last semester."

"How? When? After school, in private? Or did you challenge her in front of the class?"

Kelsey gave in with a shrug.

"You know, if I were Mrs. Delaney, I'd let the whole bunch of you fail for acting like spoiled five-year-olds!"

"A protest is a legitimate means of—"

"Sure it is," Ms. Elliot interrupted, "when grievances have been voiced and an effort has been made to reach a compromise before the protest begins. But sitting in class doing nothing isn't a protest. It's a . . . a . . . I have no idea what it is." She seemed to have run out of steam. "What I do know is that you're both in one heck of a mess."

For a long while the three stood together on the first floor landing, each lost in private thoughts. Then, as always, Ms. Elliot took charge of her athletes.

"Okay, let me tell you what you're going to do," she said, squaring her shoulders. "You are going to walk into the office, and you are going to say 'Yes, sir,' and 'No, sir,' politely, respectfully, like the well-mannered young women you are. You are not going to argue. You are not going to say another thing. You are going to gather up your belongings, go home, and think, think hard about how to end this protest before I get really mad."

She stepped forward and straightened Kelsey's hair, running her fingers through the coarse, thick waves, trying to tame them into some sense of style. Then she turned to Ratasha and gave her blouse a firm tug, pulling it down and smoothing it out. Without another word Ms. Elliot lifted her chin, took a deep breath, and walked between the girls, obviously expecting them to follow. Kelsey glanced at Ratasha, offered a nod, and the two turned to trail their coach.

The interview was formal, impersonal, like reading a prisoner his or her Miranda rights. In a matter of minutes both were informed of their suspensions and told they could not return to school without the accompaniment of a parent or guardian. A security guard was called to escort them off campus.

Humiliation didn't come close to describing Kelsey's disgrace. The guard was a police officer assigned to the high school campus, and he was Russ's friend. They'd shared classes in college, played ball on the same teams, and in all the years Kelsey had known him, Officer Gilbert always had a smile.

Not today. His simple commands—step into the hall, open your locker—were professional, emotionless, and cold. Even when she pleaded with him not to tell Russ, Officer Gilbert wouldn't comment.

By the time she got home, Kelsey felt like a tightly wound clock spring frozen in time. Years ago, after she had pulled a ridiculous stunt in junior high, Dr. Lawrence had delivered her to her father, who had taken immediate steps to see that his daughter never misbehaved at school again. After grounding her, he'd reiterated his expectations, then told her how disappointed he was in her actions. The hurt she saw in his eyes stayed with Kelsey as a constant reminder of what awaited her if she acted up again, and she had avoided trouble at school like the plague.

She had no idea how her father would have reacted to today's events. He'd always been judicious, listening to Kelsey's side of any controversy before meting out a punishment. But she wasn't dealing with her dad; she was dealing with Russ, who would probably overreact and blow the whole thing out of proportion the way he always did.

Like last fall? When you got in that fight? she asked herself. *He was fair then.*

And it was true. Four months after her father's death, Kelsey had exploded at school over some petty issue and had been sent home for the rest of the day. Russ was indeed furious but also deeply concerned because her rage was so atypical it scared them both. So he'd talked and sought help, forcing Kelsey to face her grief until her anger was dispelled. It was later he said his own words, serious words, about how he never wanted to get called up to school again.

But here she was, suspended, definitely not within Russ's range of comprehension.

Maybe Nathan would go back to school with her. Technically he wasn't her guardian, but he was listed on her emergency card, and the vice principal knew him.

It was a tempting solution. Nathan would definitely have his say, but if he could get her reinstated, Russ might not find out until—

Until when? Ms. Elliot knew, Officer Gilbert knew, and Dr. Lawrence probably did too. But not Russ, not yet. If he'd known, he'd have been over at the house and they'd be having one heck of a row right now. If only Nathan could get her back into school, she would find Mrs. Delaney and make her listen. Russ would still probably fuss, and they'd have to talk, and no doubt he'd issue another penalty or two. He might even decide to check up on her more, but that was okay. At least it would be over, and they could laugh and tease and joke and share, the way they used to before this whole mess began. She could stop by for dinner and go out with friends, and life would be normal again.

But first she had to convince Nathan to stand in for their brother. And that, Kelsey knew, would be no small task.

18

a warning from the past

A difficult hour passed before Kelsey summoned the nerve to knock on her brother's door.

"Nathan, do you have a minute?"

"Sure, sis." He grabbed the mouse and saved his work, then brought his left hand up to his neck and rubbed wearily.

"Here, let me do that," Kelsey said. She moved behind his chair and began to gently massage the muscles in his upper back. "You're really tight. You been working on the computer all day?"

"I wish. I only got home two hours ago."

"What can I do to help?"

"Fix me a sandwich." He lolled his head from side to side. "You and Russ okay?"

"Might be if you go to school with me tomorrow."

Nathan's hand flew over his shoulder, and he caught her by the wrist. "Have a seat," he said, swinging around. She settled onto his bed and scooted up toward the pillows.

"Now talk to me, Kelsey Gene. Why do you want me to go with you to school?"

Kelsey bit her lip. "I got suspended."

A look of complete incomprehension crossed her brother's face. "Excuse me?"

"They suspended five of us today for what they called disrupting the learning environment."

"And you need someone to get you reinstated."

Kelsey nodded.

"Does Russ know?"

Kelsey shook her head.

Nathan's gray eyes narrowed to an incredulous frown. "Then no way, Kelsey Gene. I'm surprised you'd even ask."

"I'm desperate here. Russ is acting strange. I don't know how he'll take this."

"Strange how?" Nathan asked, the doctor-to-be taking notice.

"Well, he grounded me when we didn't end the protest Friday. Only he didn't lecture, or fuss, or give me alternatives like he always does. He just sent me home as if he didn't want to see me anymore. Then all weekend I had to keep reporting in on the computer like I lived a thousand miles away. He hasn't asked me to dinner or anything. He's acting as if I'm a stranger, like he's just a trooper doing his job. And now, with this, I don't know what he's going to do."

"Sure you do," Nathan said, leaning back. "First he'll have his say, and then he'll ground you for what? Two months? Three? At least until you graduate. You'll miss the prom—"

"Hush!" Kelsey said. It wasn't even funny. "I get so tired of Russ telling me what to do. I can make my own decisions, and he doesn't have to treat me like a criminal because I made one he didn't like."

"We all live by rules, Kelsey Gene. I have to meet guidelines at school that sometimes seem like nothing more than an exercise in frustration. And for now, you have to get along with Russ, if for no other reason than to honor Dad because *he's* the one who made Russ your guardian."

A quick surge of anger flushed across Kelsey's face, and Nathan sat up. "I saw that, sis. You don't agree?"

"What difference does it make?" Kelsey asked. "When you bring up Dad, you cut off any possibility of discussion. How can I argue against honoring him?"

"Exactly my point," Nathan said, smiling a bit. "For the moment you are stuck, so you might as well learn to get along."

It was a small opening, but one worth pursuing.

"If you go with me, I could tell Russ about it later, and it wouldn't be so hard on him, and—"

Nathan shook his head. "From what I've read about civil disobedience, often reformation has a price."

"What are you saying?" Kelsey mumbled.

"Last week you defended your right to protest. At least you told me that you were acting on a principle that you thought was just."

"So?"

"So you should be willing to accept a little discomfort to prove the validity of your position. Russ isn't going to set you in front of a firing squad, only make you wish that he had."

Kelsey groaned.

"If, however, you've changed your mind about the worthiness of your actions, then you should end the protest immediately and accept your responsibilities."

Nathan laughed heartily at his sister's exasperated stare. "Kelsey Gene, how do you get yourself into these messes?"

"I wish I knew," she said, scooting toward the end of the bed. "You won't go with me?"

Nathan raised an eyebrow and again shook his head. "You wanted to make your own decisions, and you did. Now you have to deal with the consequences."

"Then what am I going to do?"

"First," Nathan answered, as always direct, "you're going to ask Russ to go to school with you tomorrow. Then, when you see him, you're going to listen to him, Kelsey Gene—not argue, not tell him you are right. You are going to say as little as possible except that you are sorry."

Kelsey swung her legs over the side and frowned. Apologize?

"You have a problem with that?" Nathan asked, his eyes widening in disbelief.

"I don't like apologizing to Russ."

Nathan threw up his hands. "Fine. Then don't."

He spun around on his chair and reopened his file.

Dismissed again? It was becoming a bad routine. Kelsey stood up, watching Nathan go back to his work as if she weren't even there. Why couldn't she tell Russ she was sorry? He was going to have to give up his morning to hear things he didn't want to hear, and all because she'd gotten involved in something that was fast becoming a real threat to graduation.

"And after I tell him I'm sorry?" she asked, her voice small, contrite.

"Remember he loves you."

Kelsey leaned down to give Nathan a hug. "You sure?"

"Of course. Aren't you?" he asked, patting her arm.

Kelsey nodded against Nathan's shoulder before

straightening up. "What kind of sandwich do you want?"

"A bacon, lettuce, and tomato with extra bacon."

"Heart attack city! And you have a fit if I drink a little extra coffee!"

"But not half the fit Russ is going to have when he hears you've been suspended."

"*Nathan!*"

"You asked what I *wanted*, Kelsey Gene. What I'll settle for is a tuna on toast, light on the mayo."

"Oh," she said, heading downstairs to make the sandwich. So much for the easy way out. One way or another she was going to have to face Russ.

It was after nine when she booted up her computer, hoping to leave a message and exit like a thief. At least an electronic note wouldn't shake the way her voice would over the phone, but Russ was already on-line.

Wonderful, Kelsey thought. *Why did he have to be home?* The answer wasn't important. He was.

```
Russ, I need you to go to school with me
tomorrow.


Why?


I got suspended. I can't go back to class
until you meet with Mr. Arnold.
```

After an eternal pause, a brief, detached response appeared.

```
I'll meet you in the students' lot at 7:45.
```

She glanced away, assuming the exchange was over, but the words hung on in an uneasy echo, as if trying to ward off the horror that flashed next.

```
Do you remember me saying that I didn't
ever want to hear about you getting in
trouble at school again?
```

Kelsey felt her pulse race as she fumbled with the keys.

```
Yes.
```

Russ's response danced back instantly.

```
Well, so do I!
```

Kelsey stared at the screen, wondering if she should say more, maybe something about being sorry, as Nathan had suggested; but before she could decide, Russ logged off, extinguishing her last ray of hope.

19

the morning news

Russ was waiting in the parking lot, leaning against the fender of his truck, dressed in full uniform, when Kelsey pulled in, three minutes shy of seven forty-five.

"Thanks for coming," she said as she got out. "I know it's an inconvenience, and I want you to know, you know, that I appreciate it."

"You're babbling, Kelsey Gene," he said, turning toward the school, his long stride eating up the distance between the parking lot and the main door at a frightening pace. Kelsey scrambled to keep up.

"No. I mean it, Russ. I really appreciate your help."

"The only reason I'm here is because Nathan wouldn't come. Right?"

So much for talk, Kelsey thought, dying inside. If he wouldn't listen to her here in front of the school, he'd never listen to her later at home. She was puffing as if she'd run a fast mile by the time they got to the office, and that only meant her emotions were running amok. She wasn't *that* out of shape.

Russ opened the door and stepped back, allowing her to pass through first, and an unwelcomed whoosh of cold air swirled down from the ceiling fan. Her muscles tightened, warning her to find a chair quickly, before her knees buckled, and she hustled across the room to a remote corner, where she would be out of sight from the hall. She dropped heavily in the nearest chair and drew herself in, trying to get warm.

"Good morning, Mrs. Parks," Russ said, grinning sheepishly at the secretary as he ambled over to the counter.

"Russell Blackwell! It's so good to see you!" Mrs. Parks reached forward and gave Russ her hand for a quick clasp. "Still patrolling the Old Roberts's cutoff?"

"Uh-huh. Still keeping the speed down?"

Kelsey listened to their casual exchange, inquiries about children and family, and marveled at her brother's ability with people. He could appear so relaxed that he would put the most anxious speeders at ease or, if he chose, make them wish they'd never seen a car. Within minutes the phone interrupted the small talk, reminding the secretary of her duties, and she shifted her attention to the caller. Russ turned away and leaned against the counter while he slowly studied the room, a practice Kelsey had seen him apply a thousand times, cataloging, scrutinizing, looking for anything out of place. He ended with Mrs. Parks, who was still engaged with the caller. She covered the mouthpiece.

"Mr. Arnold has someone with him," she whispered. "It will be about five minutes."

Russ nodded and for the first time looked directly into his sister's eyes, then crossed over and pressed into the corner between Kelsey's chair and the wall, standing at her side to wait.

Suddenly the door opened with a definite shove, and Terrance's mother marched in, followed by her reluctant son. Tension ballooned in the already anxious atmosphere, and Kelsey's muscles tightened even more. She tried to catch Terrance's attention, but his eyes never left the floor.

"I am Sonya Jackson," his mother announced, "and I am here to see Mr. Arnold." The proclamation was made to Mrs. Parks, who was still on the phone.

She covered the mouthpiece. "Mr. Arnold will be with you as soon as he's seen Mr. Blackwell."

She nodded toward Russ, and Sonya looked over her shoulder at her old high school friend.

"If there is anything I can do to help," he said quietly, "let me know."

"Thank you, Russell. I will." Sonya turned toward

her son. "*You!* Over there!"

She pointed to the spot Kelsey had shunned, right in front of the hall window, and Terrance took the assigned seat immediately, slumping down to rest the back of his neck against the chair, his long legs stretched out in front. His mother perched primly next to him.

"If you *ever* want to see a basketball court again, you'd better sit like you've been taught."

Terrance's spine stiffened, and he shot up, towering over his mother, who somehow still seemed the larger of the two.

Kelsey tensed even more, wanting to shout at Ms. Jackson to stop embarrassing her son, but Russ's hand settled heavily on his sister's shoulder, cautioning her to be still. She took a deep breath, and another, appreciating all the more her brother's self-control. Never had he reprimanded her in public, never in front of her friends. Even around Marti he'd take Kelsey aside, unless Marti was a culprit too. Then he treated them equally.

The sound of an opening door sent a shudder down Kelsey's back, as Mr. Juarez emerged from Mr. Arnold's office, his face glowing with anger. JJ, sober and pale, followed one step behind. Kelsey felt Russ's fingers slip down her arm, drawing her up, steering her down the corridor, into a room. Suddenly she was there, where JJ had been, and all she wanted was out.

"Thank you for coming, Officer Blackwell," the vice principal said, standing behind his desk, letting his dark suit and unsmiling eyes define the nature of the meeting. He nodded to Kelsey and motioned toward two empty chairs. "Won't you have a seat?

"We seem to have a real problem on our hands," Mr. Arnold said, waiving any further pleasantries as he took his own chair behind the desk. "Has your sister told you what's been happening in her English class?"

Russ looked at Kelsey and nodded.

"Well, Thursday the students refused to leave when the bell rang, preventing the next class from entering. It took us several minutes of valuable time to get things back to order. I'm afraid our position on this is quite clear. We understand your sister was among those who initiated the so-called protest, and this action has now become disruptive to others. We cannot allow a handful of students to destroy the learning environment for the majority. Therefore, a hearing is scheduled in ten days to determine if your sister will be allowed to continue attending school in our district."

Kelsey's blood turned to ice. Expelled? Two months before graduation?

Mr. Arnold passed a white envelope to Russ, who

opened it and read its contents before dropping it in his sister's lap. It was an official notification of the hearing.

"Do you have any questions?"

Russ's fingers were drumming slowly on his knee, a simple gesture that clawed at Kelsey's nerves, ripping apart what little composure she had left. He always sat so still, so disciplined.

He glanced sideward. "I want a word with Mr. Arnold alone. Wait by my truck."

She nodded and picked at the letter, trying to get a hold, to give it back, but her fingers wouldn't connect. Russ slipped his arm around her back and set her on her feet, using his free hand to scoop up the paper as it wafted to the floor. She looked around for the door. It had been there when she came in. Where was it now? She felt someone guide her toward the wall— oh, there was the door—taking her keys.

"Wait by the truck," Russ said again, heading her down the hall toward the lobby, and she stumbled along, one step, two, until she was finally outside, shivering in the sun. A school bus pulled into the unloading zone carrying freshmen, sophomores, kids too young to drive, and they leaped up, piling to the front, emerging from the yellow dungeon with a restless swirl. Kelsey staggered past. She couldn't even remember being that young, what, two years ago?

When she saw the Renegade, her hand slipped automatically into her pocket, searching. Oh. Never mind. Russ had her keys, and she was too weak to run away on foot, which was exactly what he was counting on.

Desperately in need of a place to sit down, she lowered the tailgate to her brother's truck, crawled up into the bed, and backed against the side to face the sun, trying to get warm. Deep breaths, slow breaths, in, out, relax, go limp.

She sensed Russ's presence before she saw him moving across the lot. He leaned against the side of the truck bed and studied his sister carefully. "You're in a lot of trouble this time, Kelsey Gene."

"I know, and I'm so sorry!" To her surprise, the words she thought would be so hard just flew out. "What'd Arnold say after I left?"

"Not much, except that you can go back to class now, and we need to take this hearing seriously. Do you realize, if Dad had lived, he'd be the one handling the proceedings against you?"

Kelsey stared at the floor, afraid if she blinked, tears would fill up her heart and she would drown.

"I need some time to think about all this. Come by the house after practice."

She scooted forward and dangled her legs over the

edge, waiting for strength.

Russ's eyes widened slightly. "What, no protest? No argument about your being too old for a guardian?"

Kelsey shook her head. "Nathan told me to keep my mouth shut."

"Then you did ask him to come with you."

"Of course! You would have too in my place."

"Maybe," Russ said, wrapping his hands around his sister's rib cage and lifting her to the ground. He slid his fingers under the tailgate, slammed it shut, and turned away. She could feel his disappointment as the now-familiar distance began to settle in like a dense fog.

"You have my keys, Russell," she said, dusting herself off.

He pulled them from his pocket and flipped them back over his head. "You run away, Kelsey Gene, and I *will* find you."

"Is that a promise or a threat?" she asked, snatching the ring from the air as it sailed by her head. She hoped it was a promise. She liked to think he wanted her in his life, even when he was really hurt.

He started the engine and backed out, waiting until he was alongside Kelsey before answering. "That, my dear sister, is a fact. Have a good day."

She watched him drive off, looking tired and tense. A good day? Now how on earth was she ever going to do that? She turned toward the Renegade.

I could cut, she thought as she unlocked the door and reached across the passenger seat to get her gym bag. *I could get in, drive away, and hide.*

And the school would call, and Russ would find her, and . . .

She spun away, slamming the door, afraid if she hung around, she would obey that inane thought. In reality, she was in a mess. In reality, it wasn't going away. In reality, Russ was at the edge of his patience. And in reality, she had no choice but to go inside, muddle though this day, and hope that by its end she had something good to tell.

20

day six

Kelsey took a small bite of her sandwich and glanced around. Everyone at the table was quiet, as if the simple act of chewing needed complete concentration. It had not been a good twenty-four hours. Mr. Arnold's talk with the class had had a sobering effect on those not suspended, causing a rift in solidarity. Some wanted to end the protest immediately, but others felt that to do so without first getting Mrs. Delaney to forgive their zeros would be to lose. No one could agree, and English was less than ten minutes away.

As if it even mattered. Kelsey had spent much of the night and most of the morning trying to figure out who had told Mr. Arnold she'd been one of the leaders in starting the protest. Hadn't it more or less started on a whim? At lunch one day? Hadn't everyone agreed?

She couldn't even remember who had been the first one to mention it, but it certainly hadn't been her, and she didn't think it was JJ, Ratasha, or Terrance. Drew? Maybe, but what if he had? No one had voiced an objection or refused to join in. Until Mr. Arnold got an attitude yesterday, everyone had been tight.

There was the distinct possibility that no one had said anything, that it was all just a bluff by the administration, a ploy to tear them apart.

Whatever. It was definitely working.

"So what are we going to do?" JJ asked the group in general, and a buzz started around the table, with everyone saying the same things over and over again. If they continued the demonstration and were expelled, they would lose credit in all classes, not just one. But to give in could mean to fail English. One student suggested calling the media, insisting that the administration would take a whole different path if its actions were spotlighted in the press. Others were not ready for such a drastic step. Drew suggested they go in and continue as before. He was the only one suspended whose parents had not levied penalties, and although some still sided with him, those who had the most to lose—Kelsey, JJ, Ratasha, and Terrance—emphatically said no. Others wanted to sue the school on grounds of discrimination, and the possibilities degenerated from there.

Kelsey wrapped up her half-eaten sandwich, which

held all the appeal of cardboard, and sighed heavily. They were getting nowhere, and she was tired of trying to think for a group. She leaned her head toward Ratasha.

"What do you think?"

Ratasha looked at her without a trace of a smile. "I think my parents are *real* upset. You figured out who said we started it?"

Kelsey shook her head. "No, and I don't think I even care. I'm not going to class."

"You're what?" JJ said, overhearing.

"I'm going to cut," Kelsey whispered. It was an idea that had been haunting her ever since she left Russ in the parking lot.

Ratasha and JJ both were at a loss for words.

"Look," Kelsey said, trying not to attract attention, "I don't want to go sit in class for another fifty-five minutes doing nothing. It drives me crazy, but neither do I want to mess up the protest. So I'm going to the gym and ask Ms. Elliot if I can hang out there."

"Won't that be putting her on the spot?" JJ asked.

"Maybe. But since we have a sub for Delaney again, it should be okay." She smiled wryly. "At least then no one can say I am making them protest."

Ratasha nodded. "This is a good idea. If we don't go to class, we aren't interfering with the process. But then no one can call us the leaders either."

"Hey, I don't think I said 'we,'" Kelsey remarked.

"No, it's a good idea, Kelsey Gene," JJ said, nodding to himself. "I could go to Mr. Lazoya's, and Terrance could go to Coach Mobly's. Let the others follow Drew's lead."

"It will look like we're still protesting if we all cut—"

"But that's okay," Ratasha interrupted. "The basic issue is the same. We are still failing English, and we have to get this settled before we end the strike."

"We'll just be demonstrating in a different way."

The electronic trill of the bell brought a close to the conversation.

"Then we're all in this for one more day?" Drew asked.

Heads nodded as legs swung over the bench, and there was a general scramble to be gone. JJ laid a hand on Terrance's arm.

"Wait up," he said, and Terrance stopped while JJ shouldered his backpack.

"Tell you what," Kelsey said, watching the guys walk away together, Terrance leaning slightly toward JJ as if trying to catch each word. "I'm going to tell Elliot it was all your idea."

"You do," Ratasha said matter-of-factly, "and Elliot

will be the least of your troubles."

Kelsey laughed. They'd been dissing each other for years, and somehow the exchange felt good, almost as if things were returning to normal.

"How do you think I should approach her?" Kelsey asked.

"Simple. Fall on the floor and beg for mercy."

It took only three of the allowed five minutes to hustle across the basketball court, through the locker room, and down the damp hall to Ms. Elliot's office. Kelsey stuck her head through the open door.

"Ms. Elliot? May we have a word with you?"

The coach looked up startled and then motioned them in.

"We've decided not to go to class, and we were wondering, you know, if we could stay here."

Ms. Elliot slapped her palm against her forehead. "I don't believe this! You are cutting class?"

"No, ma'am," Kelsey said. "You know where we are, so we are not cutting. We are assisting another teacher."

"Me? I didn't send for you."

"Oh, we must have misunderstood," Ratasha said, taking up where Kelsey left off. The tardy bell sounded, marking the beginning of the next class. "Would you mind, though, if we stayed? We'd be late for class anyway."

"Oh, I mind," Ms. Elliot commented, coming to life. "But I'll tell you what I'll do."

She opened the lower-left-hand desk drawer and came out with two packets, one with Kelsey's name, one with Ratasha's. "Seems I was able to get the work you've not been doing in English class lately."

She spread the folders out on the desk in front of the girls. "So I will let you stay here as long as you work on these assignments. I'll be back in fifty minutes, and you'd better have something to show for the time." She pushed herself off the desk and quickly left the room, shutting the door on her way out.

Ratasha's fingers rifled through the pages. "There must be thirty papers here."

"At least," Kelsey said, hunting through her literature book for the first assigned story. "I wonder if everyone is still following Drew's lead."

"Who cares?" Ratasha replied as they got busy.

Ms. Elliot returned at the end of the hour and checked over their work. "You will spend your athletic period the same way," she commented, apparently satisfied that her athletes had taken the assignments seriously. "And since you'll be missing the conditioning, you will run the bases twenty extra times after practice to stay in shape." She turned and walked out, leaving the girls to pack up.

Kelsey slipped the folder into her bag. "Let's try

to do the first three tonight and compare our ideas tomorrow."

"Sounds good," Ratasha said, hoisting her pack to her shoulder. "See ya at practice. I gotta run."

Kelsey fumbled with her belongings, hurrying, trying to rush out before Ms. Elliot caught her alone, but the coach stepped through the door seconds after Ratasha left.

"Did Russell or Nathan come with you this morning?"

"Russ," Kelsey answered, a little surprised. She just assumed that Elliot and her brother had spoken.

"And you're still alive?"

"I'm supposed to meet him after school to learn my fate," she replied, watching Ms. Elliot's face. "Send flowers if I'm not here tomorrow."

"You'll get no sympathy from me on this one, Blackwell," the coach barked, and Kelsey's mouth settled into a crooked grin.

"No, ma'am. I didn't expect that I would."

"Russ left a message for me to call," Ms. Elliot went on. "I'll have to be honest with him. I think this whole thing is ridiculous."

"Yes, ma'am. As soon as Mrs. Delaney gets back, we're going to talk to her, work something out," Kelsey said. "Thanks for getting the assignments."

Ms. Elliot smiled slightly and nodded. "You can show me your appreciation by getting yourself out of this mess."

She turned and left, muttering about how she was going to call the coach at the university and warn her to beware of a certain redheaded hockey player who'd been given a scholarship. Kelsey warmed to the words. For the first time it felt like the beginning of a possible end. At least Ms. Elliot had been willing to listen to them and help.

If only Russ could step back a little and see that his sister was searching for a graceful way out, not trying deliberately to ruin her life. If only he would listen before he made his decision to do whatever it was he was going to do.

Russ always listens to you, Kelsey told herself. *He just doesn't always agree.*

And when he didn't, it wasn't Kelsey's view that prevailed. Like it or not, in less than four hours she would be standing in front of her brother, he'd be having his say, and all she could do was accept his decision.

21

facts of life

It was almost six-thirty by the time Kelsey finished her punishment laps, packed up her gym bag, and drove to her brother's house. As before, the light was on in Russ's shop: not a good sign. When he was alone with his projects, his mind sometimes wandered to their dad, and at the moment the thing that worried Kelsey the most was that her brother's loyalty to their father might cloud his judgment. Silently, unwillingly, she moved from the Jeep to the shop, and settled onto the watcher's stool.

"You're late, Kelsey Gene," Russ said, sensing her presence without turning around. Three seconds. A new record.

"Ms. Elliot made me run extra bases."

"I'm not even going to ask why."

A new undercurrent played in his voice: not anger but something else, a tone of determination, or was it resignation? Kelsey studied the back of his head, wondering what he was thinking as he worked a clamp onto the corner of the Victorian frame. All day she'd dreaded this moment, envisioned it a thousand times, but always without an ending.

"Russ, I—"

He held up his hand for her to hush, then walked purposefully out the door, motioning to her to follow, and she slid down, mentally grumbling. Follow, follow, follow: Was that all she did? Why couldn't she just this once say, "No, I'm not going anywhere. We will talk here." Did she have no backbone? No courage?

Suddenly she stopped, feet sticking to the earth, resisting any forward motion. Russ was heading to the picnic table, a replica of the one at home. How many times had she sat across from him, debating, arguing, learning to listen? Their dad had jokingly built Russ this table when Megan, the image of an infant Kelsey Gene, was born. And if this is where her brother wanted to talk, he was in one heck of a mood.

She forced herself forward and sat down on the bench opposite Russ, who was already settled.

"This will be brief, Kelsey Gene," he said, leaning forward on his elbows. "I've gone back and forth on what to do, asked myself what Dad would have done. I suspect he would have found a way to stop you before

157

things had escalated this far. Hindsight is always perfect, and I realize now that I should have acted last week: pulled you out of honors or forced a meeting with Mrs. Delaney.

"So I will assume some of the responsibility for the way this situation has developed, but not much. It's been your chosen action, or perhaps I should say nonaction, that has led to the hearing."

He pulled several business-size envelopes from his shirt pocket, each with a number, and fanned them out on the table.

"I cannot allow you, a Blackwell, to tarnish Daddy's memory in the same boardroom where he was so respected. You have exactly four chances to end this nonsense, Kelsey Gene."

He arranged the envelopes in numerical order.

"And to help keep you focused, I have come up with five different consequences, one for each day you choose not to be considerate enough of Mrs. Delaney to go into her English class and do the assigned work."

Five? Kelsey wondered. But hadn't he said "four chances"?

"Because," Russ said, sensing her unasked question, "what is written in the fifth envelope will end your involvement, and that *is* a fact." He waited for his words to sink in, then pushed envelope number one forward. "Open it."

Kelsey fumbled with the tab, not even trying to hide her shaking hands, and read the message:

YOU ARE GROUNDED FOR ONE FULL WEEK.

A week. She could handle a week. But what was in number two and three? Why was he so sure number five would work?

Russ gathered up the other four envelopes and stuck them in his hip pocket. "That's all, Kelsey Gene. Go home, and check in on the computer every half hour."

"Russ, I—"

"I said that was all!"

An edge of pink invaded Russ's cheeks, and Kelsey stood quickly. She wanted to say she was sorry, that she was trying to figure out a solution, that she was doing her work, but now wasn't the time for talk. She took one step, then another. *Don't cry, not yet.* Pride called for control, complete, total control until she was out of her brother's sight.

His speech had been so precise, so rehearsed, as if he had been afraid to lose his tightly maintained composure. In some ways Kelsey admired his ability to restrain his emotions; in other ways it frightened her. She didn't know this cold Russell, and she didn't want to. She hated the distance he had created between them. Always before they'd been a unit, separate individuals—Russ, Nathan, and Kelsey—connected by an inseparable bond. But now this stupid protest was tearing them apart.

She hated it, hated it, hated it!

The protest didn't seem to be the real issue at all anymore. It had been overshadowed by something deeper and far more personal.

Kelsey fingered the envelope in her hand. Number one. Grounding. Check your computer. Number five will end—what was it he had said? "What is written in the fifth envelope will end *your* involvement."

How? Kelsey wondered as she reached into her pocket for her keys. And deep inside she knew that was one thing she hoped she would never find out.

22

reasons why

Kelsey heard the phone ringing in the house seconds after she switched off the ignition. All the way home she'd replayed the scene at the picnic table—Russ's refusal to listen, his flushed cheeks—and she was seething. Who did he think he was anyway, cutting her off like that? She had as much right to talk as he did, and it was high time *he* learned to listen. She grabbed her gym bag and flew into the house, barely managing to snatch up the receiver before the call switched over to the answering service.

"Damn it, Russell! At least give me enough time to get in the door!"

The pause was so long, Kelsey thought he'd hung up, and that was just fine! She'd heard enough about envelopes and computer check-ins and number five's ending it all. It was her future, her life, her—

"I know you've been taught to answer more politely

than that, Kelsey Gene." Air rushed into her lungs as if pushed by an invisible compressor. "Would you please try again?"

"Yes, sir," she answered with what little voice she could find. "Hello?"

"Hello, Kelsey Gene. This is Jim Lawrence. Do you have a minute?"

"Yes, sir." Kelsey collapsed onto the floor and leaned back against the cabinet.

"That's much better," Dr. Lawrence went on. His voice sounded more encouraging than angry. "You and Russ must be having one heck of a row."

Kelsey sighed, releasing the strain on her throat. "He had to go to school today to see Mr. Arnold."

"Then I'm glad I'm not in your shoes. I'll bet he's furious."

"You know Russ."

"Unfortunately, I don't think what I have to say is going to make your day any better."

Kelsey tucked her knees up to her chest and gathered herself in. "What is it?"

"I've found out why Mrs. Delaney has stopped teaching this semester, and I don't know any easy way to say this. Her husband is dying, Kelsey Gene, from pancreatic cancer. There isn't anything that can be done."

"Oh, no," Kelsey said, feeling an all-too-familiar rush of sadness grip her heart. "I had no idea."

"Not very many people have," Dr. Lawrence said. "Mrs. Delaney is a *very* private person."

Suddenly a new picture of Mrs. Delaney emerged, of someone struggling with prolonged grief, with the pain of impending separation. Kelsey's father had died instantly, but occasionally, when she was alone in the night, she wondered if it would have been easier if she'd had a chance to say good-bye.

"From what I've been told," Dr. Lawrence was saying, "she's been carrying quite a load. None of their family is close by, so she has been nursing him at night, juggling medical appointments during the day, and at the same time dealing with her own emotions."

"That's rough," Kelsey said, trying to think things through. "I don't know what to say."

"Me either," Dr. Lawrence replied. "Apparently when she first learned of her husband's diagnosis, she went to the principal and asked Dr. Martin to relieve her of the AP class. She felt that considering the circumstances, she wouldn't have the emotional energy to be consistently challenging."

"But nothing changed," Kelsey commented, wondering why.

"Well, it seems when Dr. Martin went to the faculty,

no one would step forward to help. So he told Mrs. Delaney that if she resigned her AP class, she'd be let go."

"Can he do that?"

"Her contract does read that she cannot resign from one part of her teaching assignment without sacrificing her whole job. It wasn't the compassionate thing to do, but it was legal."

"But why wouldn't anyone help?" Kelsey asked. She'd never heard anything negative about members of the English department except maybe that they gave too much homework.

"Oh, they all had what they thought were good reasons: their own families, lack of AP certification. Advanced classes do take special training and more preparation. One agreed to take a sophomore class, and someone else offered to grade papers, but Mrs. Delaney was hurt that there wasn't a bigger show of support. So she told them not to bother, she'd handle things herself. Mr. Marshall is the only one certified for AP at the junior/senior level, and he was willing to help. But he's already teaching three different classes, and the school board requires notification when a teacher is assigned four preparations. Dr. Martin didn't want to get them involved."

"Well, they're involved now," Kelsey said.

"There's a hearing scheduled in ten days to review our disruptive behavior."

"Is that why Russ was called to school?"

"Oh, yeah," Kelsey said, almost singing the words.

"Why don't you tell me what happened?"

"The usual." Kelsey began but she had a hard time shifting her thoughts away from Mrs. Delaney. "We talked, or maybe I should say that Russell talked. I listened."

She went on to tell about the picnic table, the five envelopes, and Russ's declaration that the protest, or at least Kelsey's part in the protest, would end before the hearing.

"I don't like the sound of that, Kelsey Gene," Dr. Lawrence said when she finished.

"Neither do I. Any ideas?"

"No, but I think I'll pay your brother a visit."

"Thanks," she said. As her father's closest friend Jim Lawrence had a strong influence over both her brothers. He might be just the person to bring Russ to his senses.

"You know, Kelsey Gene, Mrs. Delaney doesn't need added stress in her life right now. Would it be so hard to walk into class, pick up your pen, and get to work?"

"I wish I could, Dr. Lawrence," she said, searching for a way to make him understand. "But I don't want to fail, and until Mrs. Delaney agrees to let us make up the work, we've got to stick to the original plan. We haven't had a chance to talk to her, because she's been absent, but we're going to, as soon as she gets back. Meanwhile Russ is having a fit. I'm in a lose-lose situation."

"Perhaps, but who do you think is suffering the real loss here, you or Mrs. Delaney?"

"I know she is hurting," Kelsey replied, "and we *are* going to talk to her as soon as she gets back to school."

"Good. Now how about if you come over for a while? I could round up Marti and Ruth. We could play some two-on-two."

"Sorry," Kelsey said. "I'm grounded—big time. Russ makes me report in every half hour on the computer."

A chuckle of approval filtered through the receiver. "Now that's a novel approach."

Kelsey didn't answer. She didn't dare say out loud what she was thinking, at least not within earshot of Dr. Lawrence.

"If you need anything, will you call?" he asked.

"Yes, sir."

"Remember Ruth and I love you. Try to get a good night's sleep."

"I will. Thanks."

Sleep. That would be a miracle, Kelsey thought as she hung up. *And if I don't check in with Russell, he'll come unglued.*

She grabbed her gym bag and trudged upstairs, exhausted. How long had it been since she slept a solid eight hours? Not since last Monday, before this whole mess began.

She booted up the computer and reported in.

```
I'm home, Russell.
```

```
Do I need to make an appointment for you
with Dr. Krammar?
```

So he had noticed how upset she was when she left. Dr. Krammar was the grief counselor they'd visited, individually and collectively, when their mother disappeared into her depression after their father's death, and he was one of the few people Kelsey would talk to openly.

```
No. I'm okay.
```

```
How do you know?
```

```
Because I cussed you all the way home!
```

It was a long time before the next message appeared.

Check in again at 8:22.

Kelsey laughed. Russ's pause was all she needed to know her words had gotten a reaction. Maybe he was hiding behind the computer, but he wasn't as detached as he wanted her to believe.

She glanced at the bed. She could fix a sandwich before the next scheduled contact, or she could lie down and rest.

Better not, she warned herself. *You'll sleep until morning, and you have way too much homework for that.*

She pulled her literature book and folder out of her gym bag and checked her next assignment. Then she piled a mound of pillows against the headboard and propped herself up in bed.

Mrs. Delaney's lesson was based on Alfred, Lord Tennyson's lyrical tribute "In Memoriam." The poem expressed the raw emotions of heartache as Tennyson struggled to make sense of a friend's early death from a ruptured aneurysm. Included with the lesson was an article on the stages of grief, which Mrs. Delaney asked be applied to the poem in a written essay of no less that five hundred words.

Aneurysm.

The same thing that had taken her father.

She scooted down, trying to push half-formed thoughts away before they surfaced with fresh pain.

Concentrate on the style, she told herself as she read on. *Notice his use of sensory images.*

She read the lyrics, then picked up the article, but she gave up after a few paragraphs. It reminded her too much of her own grief, of her brothers' insistence that she talk to them, share with them. How she missed them now! She loved Nathan's quiet insight and gentle wisdom. He could home in on what was bothering her even before she knew herself. But Russ—his smile, his understanding, his approval— was the closest thing she had to a father left on this earth. She didn't want to lose him too. She didn't want to look up someday in the distant future and wonder when the connection had slipped away. If only she knew exactly what was causing his withdrawal. It had to be more than the protest. He'd never needed "distance" to punish her before. He would simply make a decision and then follow through. He would fuss and fume, and she'd have to listen, but then he'd hug her, and it would all be over. Whatever was bothering him had to be bigger than what was happening at school, something scaring him, something new.

But what? Without an answer there was no way she could be sure the distance would ever close. The feeling of separation was becoming a constant ache, begging for attention, desperate not to be ignored. One way or another she would have to find out what was going on in her brother's mind, make him talk, in words, not brief electronic messages. And once she did, she hoped life would be normal again, the way it had been a week ago, before the protest began.

23

night worries

As a child Kelsey had occasionally played in the board-room at the administration building while her father met with various authorities to discuss state law, and she loved its atmosphere. The raised platform where the school board conducted its business was surrounded by beige paneling and muted ginger carpeting that lent a cozy, earthy feel to the space. Floral pictures adorned the wall, and knickknacks made from woods and natural fabrics were spread artfully around. While her father worked, Kelsey would roam around the room, her imagination soaring with images of super-heroes saving the world.

She'd always loved this room and its memories—that is, until today. Now it felt cold and sterile. Russ, dressed in full uniform, sat to her right, Ms. Jackson and Terrance were to her left, and scattered down a long table were Ratasha and her parents, JJ and his.

One by one the school board members entered and took their seats.

Strange, Kelsey thought. Somehow she'd expected more fanfare—the media, a lawyer—not a small group of parents sitting with their children, shoulder to shoulder, facing a group of strangers talking about how to tell when potatoes were done.

And where was Drew?

The secretary entered, took her place at a small desk, and the president cleared his throat.

"We are gathered here tonight," he said, "to determine the fate of these four students who are accused of disrupting the learning environment of the school. What say ye?"

What say ye? Determine the fate? Four? Hadn't there been five who had been suspended?

"My son would like to speak." Sonya Jackson rose, yanking Terrance to his feet.

"The chair recognizes Terrance Jackson."

"She made me do it." Without turning he pointed to the right, directly at Kelsey.

"Terrance!" Kelsey protested.

"It is true," JJ yelled, jumping to his feet. "It was all her idea."

Kelsey gasped, and the room began to spin.

"We followed her lead!" Ratasha cried, joining the others.

"*M-m-my* lead?" Kelsey stammered, as her anger erupted. "What about—"

Russ leaned heavily against Kelsey, reminding her to be still, and she fought back her words.

A buzz swept through the boardroom and began to swell with bits and pieces of conversation. *Raised better than that. Wouldn't her father be ashamed? Her brother's fault. She's probably crazy, like her mom!*

The gavel came down hard again, and again, and again, crashing against the walls. "ORDER! I WILL HAVE ORDER OR THE ROOM WILL BE CLEARED!"

The room quieted, and the president looked straight at Russ. "Trooper Blackwell?"

"Sir?" he responded, his voice cold, emotionless.

"Please take your sister out."

Russ rose with wooden obedience and tucked a folder under his elbow. A scarlet *G* was clearly visible, printed neatly on the tab to the left of Kelsey's name.

"Wait!" she cried as she felt her brother's strong fingers wrap around her upper arm. "I haven't had a chan—"

"You've had plenty of chances, Kelsey Gene." The words sounded tunneled and dull, as if spoken by rote. Russ moved forward, dragging Kelsey along, and she searched the gallery as she staggered by. Spectators were jammed everywhere, on the floor, in the back, sitting, standing. She found a pocket of familiar faces—Ms. Elliot, the Lawrences, Marti—huddled in the corner, shaking their heads in reproach. Her eyes raced across the rows, hunting, hoping, stopping. Directly behind the defendants' table sat Drew, wearing a triumphant smile.

Kelsey jerked hard, but Russ tightened his hold, walking even faster, ducking his head as he stepped though a small door behind the raised platform. A dim light sent a soft yellow beam into the hall, and he swung Kelsey around front, moving her ahead. Someone was waiting, hidden in the shadows, someone she knew, needed, loved.

"Hello, Kelsey Gene."

"Daddy!" she cried, rushing forward. "I thought you were dead!"

He held out his arms, and Kelsey flung herself into the embrace, squeezing until her muscles ached before letting go.

"Why didn't you tell me he was alive?" she asked, shifting around, seeking her brother. He stood to the side, now dressed in knickers and knee socks.

"Russell has been a bad boy, Kelsey Gene. He has let you ruin your life. Now you must come with me."

Fear swept over Kelsey's body, sucking her breath away, and she pushed back.

Her father's form shifted, altering into something she no longer knew. Eyes, once warm and brown, were mustard yellow, stark, wild. Skin, once ruddy and clear, was sallow, abscessed. Kelsey pivoted as the demon grabbed her shoulders, and they collapsed to the floor, kicking, groaning, scratching until a hand clamped over her mouth. Instantly she opened wide, seeking a hold, and the hand withdrew. She took a deep breath, wondering if it were her last, and screamed.

"Ssh . . . ssh . . ."

Kelsey's eyes popped open. The room was dark. Someone was holding her, someone big. She took another breath and screamed again, shrinking as the shrill sound filled the room.

"Ssh, nothing's going to hurt you. It's only a dream."

A dream? All of it a dream? Then her father was still dead? Kelsey's body went limp, and her head crashed against a soft cotton sweater. Nathan released her shoulders and slipped his arms down her back, drawing her in close.

Still dead.

A primal sob emerged, followed by a rush of tears, and Kelsey cried long and hard, unable to control her despair. Twice she stopped, only to begin again until finally exhaustion dulled her pain. She rested against

Nathan's shoulder, feeling his strong fingers knead her back as she listened to him breathe.

"All done?" he asked, pushing a strand of dank hair out of her face. Kelsey nodded, numbed by the eruption. All she could think of was sleep.

"Want to talk about it?" Nathan's voice was quiet, soft, covering the undertow of the words.

She shook her head. She was tired, so tired.

"I think you should."

"Noooooooooo." Kelsey pulled away with a sudden twist, and retreated back against the headboard, wrapping herself in a blanket that had been thrown aside in her struggles. "Don't make me. Please?"

Nathan didn't move.

"Please? I don't need to talk, and it's over, and I feel better, so there isn't anything else to say. Really. It was nothing." She was rambling, avoiding, hiding, panicking—and they both knew it.

Nathan picked up her right hand and studied it carefully. "Do you remember the time you were playing in Russ's shop and you got a splinter right here?" He pointed to Kelsey's thumb, and she nodded. "And you didn't tell anyone because you thought it would hurt when it was dug out?"

Kelsey closed her eyes. She knew where he was headed. The splinter had festered and inflamed the whole hand.

"Nightmares are like that, Kelsey Gene. If you don't let them out, recognize where they come from, they tend to eat away at you inside."

Kelsey drew her knees to her chest and lowered her head.

"I understand that you don't want to talk, and I know that it will hurt some when you do, but telling me about the dream now may keep it from coming back."

"Please?"

"Would you rather deck me?" he asked. It was a subtle reminder, not a joke. Caught up in anger after her father's death, she'd once taken a swing at Nathan.

She peeked over her knees and smiled weakly. "Maybe."

Nathan raised his eyebrows. "I might hit back this time, and you'd still have to tell me your dream."

Kelsey groaned. He wasn't going to give in.

"Trust me on this, sis," he coaxed, his voice soothing and gentle.

"It's my only choice?" she asked, and watched him smile. Choices were Russ's thing, not Nathan's.

He looked at the ceiling as if hunting an alternative, then grinned mischievously. "You could tell Dr. Krammar."

Kelsey shook her head. She liked Dr. Krammar, but he would undoubtedly need to see her a few times, and she didn't want to go through that again. She knew her father was dead. She didn't need to keep talking about it, talking and talking. Nathan was by far the better option. He'd cut to the chase and be done.

"Or Russ."

"Oh, my God." Kelsey bolted off the bed. "What time is it?"

"Nine-thirty."

"I was supposed to report in at seven something," she mumbled. Her hands were so clumsy it took two tries to boot up. A short e-mail was waiting:

```
Check in after school tomorrow.
```

"That's it? No 'Where have you been?' No 'why haven't you kept in contact?'" She looked at Nathan, who was watching her closely. "I'd look around the room if I were you, sis."

Kelsey frowned in confusion. Nothing had changed. Her book was by her pillow, her shoes were on the floor, the blanket—

Wait. She hadn't turned the covers down. The blanket was one from the linen closet, and only three people knew the security codes to the house: Russ, Nathan, and Kelsey.

"Did you?" Kelsey asked, pointing to the bed.

"Nope. I was home only a few minutes when I heard you scream."

"I don't believe this," Kelsey sputtered, spinning around. Russ had been in her room, checking on her like a toddler!

Nathan laughed out loud. "Looks like you've recovered."

"Recovered! I've never been so furious in my life. What right does he have to come in here—"

"Hey, it's not like you've never run on him before."

She hesitated.

"And he did cover you up."

"Hush," Kelsey said, logging off. "I'm going to get something to eat."

She stomped off toward the door.

"Fix two of whatever it is," Nathan called after her. "I'm starved, and the kitchen's a great place to talk."

Wonderful, Kelsey thought as she resigned herself to the fact that before the night was over, Nathan would indeed know every detail of her dream. He wasn't about to give up, but now that the episode was more distant, she almost welcomed his insistence. Maybe he could make some sense out of what it meant.

One thing for sure, she didn't want a rerun. This

thing at school had obviously affected her more than she realized. Maybe she should drop out and repeat her senior year.

If I quit now, the failure won't show on my permanent record, Kelsey thought. *I could start again next fall and play another hockey season under Ms. Elliot and graduate with Marti.*

Maybe the coach at the university would even offer her another scholarship.

Of course Kelsey wasn't eighteen, so Russ would have to give his consent. That would definitely be a problem, but it wasn't something she had to deal with today. Now all she wanted was to put food in her stomach, do a little homework, and get a decent night's sleep. She could work on Russ later, convince him that she was in a no-win situation, tomorrow, after she'd thought things through, after tonight, after she'd told Nathan her dream.

24

negotiations

Negotiate! If Kelsey heard that word one more time, she'd scream. No, she'd go wake up Nathan, then scream in his ear. It had been his incessant theme last night, after they'd had a good laugh at the image of their six-foot-three-inch brother in knickers. Nathan had seen the nightmare as evidence that the protest was festering in Kelsey's subconscious, but he wouldn't even entertain the possibility of her dropping out of school. That was the difference between her two brothers. Russ would rave and fume; Nathan just said no.

All morning Kelsey had seen reminders of his not-so-subtle efforts to persuade, notes taped all over the house—on the mirror in the bathroom, on the refrigerator door, even on the windshield on the Renegade—with one word: *negotiate*.

Negotiate. Negotiate. NEGOTIATE.

If only she knew how.

If only . . . if only . . . *if only*. . . .

If only her mind would be quiet and leave her alone.

It was just before seven and she was already at school, sitting alone in her car, waiting for the day to finally begin, but anything beat running into another of Nathan's notes. She flipped the key over to engage the electrical system, then opened the glove box and dug through her CDs. Surely she had something to take her mind off English, something soft and soothing. A flash of maroon crossed the edge of her vision, and she lifted her head. She should have known.

JJ roared into the slot next to her, cut his engine, and held up a sixteen-ounce cup of 7-Eleven coffee. He grinned sheepishly and nodded toward the passenger seat. Kelsey grabbed her keys from the ignition and got out.

"Hey," he said, moving his books from the floor to the back so she had room to stretch out her legs, "why did I know you'd be here?"

"Because your life is as miserable as mine," Kelsey growled, rolling down the window. It was going to be a hot, steamy day.

"Big Red giving you trouble?"

Kelsey peeled back the lid of the offered treat. "Cut the shit, JJ. Russ is pissed as hell, and so's your dad."

JJ laughed. "You're right about that!"

"So how long are you grounded?" Kelsey asked, taking a big sip.

JJ sighed. "Let's say I won't have to worry about a blind date for a long, long time."

Kelsey knew the feeling. Somehow it seemed Russ was just getting warmed up to whatever he had planned.

They spent the next ten minutes talking about Dr. Lawrence's phone call and restrictions and parents and frustrations. Kelsey ended with a brief description of Nathan's early-morning notes, producing one she'd jammed into her pocket.

"He is a good thinker, Kelsey Gene. Maybe he has a point," JJ commented after he'd unwrinkled the page.

"Could be, but I have no idea what to do with it. I would never have gotten involved with this protest if I'd known Mrs. Delaney's problems, but now, with all my zeros, I feel stuck."

JJ hunted over the visor for a pen. "When I took that business management course, we had a unit on negotiation. The key is to find out what both parties want and what both are willing to give. Then you figure a way to make each think that he has won."

He drew two columns down the back of the crumpled page and headed one "Class" and the other "Mrs. Delaney."

"Okay. Now what do we want?" He quickly listed

the reason they had begun the protest: Have Mrs. Delaney return to active teaching.

"I think you need to add 'Not fail senior English,'" Kelsey said.

JJ nodded as he wrote. "Now what?"

"Cancel the school board hearing."

"Good," JJ said. He moved his pen across the page. "Okay. Now for Mrs. Delaney's side. What does she want?"

"For her husband to live?"

"We can't fix that," JJ answered softly, "though I wish we could."

Under Mrs. Delaney's name they wrote "An end to the protest," under which they subcategorized the main points: a resumption of student participation and returning control of the classroom to the teacher. Somehow, though, the words lacked clout.

"We are missing something here," JJ said. "Let's brainstorm."

He turned the paper over to the other side, where Nathan's reminder to negotiate was printed in bright red ink. JJ drew a circle in the center of the page and wrote the word "needs" inside.

"Okay. Now what did you need last fall when your mom was sick?"

"Sleep."

JJ drew another circle, wrote the word "sleep," and joined the two by a straight line.

"Hey," Kelsey said, her forehead wrinkling in disbelief, "I was kidding."

"No, you did need sleep. I remember. Mr. Marshall had to wake you up." He drew another circle. "What else was hard?"

"Well, I needed someone to talk to, but that was my own fault because I didn't tell anyone. And I remember being afraid when she was alone. I wanted someone to stay with her."

JJ wrote "talk" and "sitter" in other circles, and connected them to the one labeled "needs."

"What else?" he asked.

"I talked to Nathan last night, and he told me all the stuff Mrs. Delaney is facing. She probably has to feed her husband and bathe him. I remember with Mom it was like the work never got done, the washing, cooking, keeping up the yard, paying the bills, all the stuff Dad used to do."

JJ wrote fast.

"You know," Kelsey went on, sighing heavily, "sometimes I got lonely because things had changed so much, only I didn't have time to think about it because Mom needed care. It would have been comforting to have someone around."

JJ stuck the pen behind his ear and bounced around. "I think we have something here." He was squirming with such excitement that Kelsey felt her own hope surge. "As far as I can see, about all we have to offer is our sincere and humble apology, and time. But that's just what Mrs. Delaney needs, our time!"

"I'm not sure I'm with you," Kelsey said.

"Well, say I cooked up a great Mexican dinner and took it by for supper. Mrs. Delaney would have more time for herself."

Kelsey was beginning to catch on. "And I could clean, or sit with her husband, or mow the lawn."

"You could grade her sophomore compositions, Kelsey Gene, while I mow the lawn."

"Chauvinist!" Kelsey exclaimed.

"No, I'm no good at grading comps."

The ideas were racing, faster than the two could spill them out. Suddenly JJ grabbed Kelsey's face and kissed her squarely on the lips.

"Sorry," he said. "I had to!"

Kelsey grabbed his face and kissed him back. "I understand." She laughed.

The ten-minute warning bell sounded, summoning them to reality. Kelsey took the list and folded it with care.

"I'll talk to Ms. Elliot, see if she'll let me work on this during my athletics class. You find Terrance, see what he's willing to do. I'll catch Ratasha."

JJ nodded as they got out. Kelsey crossed over to the Renegade, picked up her gym bag, and they quickly headed for the school.

"I kind of liked that kiss," JJ said when they'd reached the girls' gym.

"JJ, you'd like a kiss from my aunt Lou," Kelsey declared, unwilling to admit she'd rather enjoyed it too.

"Is she as pretty as you?" he asked, and in spite of her best effort to be cool, Kelsey turned red.

JJ laughed heartily. "See ya at lunch."

She waved good-bye with more enthusiasm than she'd felt for days. JJ's idea was great. If she, Ratasha, JJ, Terrance, and anyone else who wanted could do some chores, Mrs. Delaney would have time to prepare her lessons, if not with the same zeal, at least with the same sincerity as last semester. And if they agreed to do their work and make up past work, the protest would be effectively ended, the school board's action nullified, and their teacher would know that they cared.

If only—

No! Kelsey shouted to herself. This time she didn't want to think of conditions and prerequisites and demands. She didn't want to consider what might go wrong. She only wanted to hope that this time, for once, everything would be okay.

25

ups and downs

Even though Mrs. Delaney was absent again, the morning passed quickly as ideas flowed into a concrete plan. Kelsey caught Ms. Elliot before school, and the coach gave a cheer when she heard the news. By lunch commitments had been made and the text finalized. Everyone, even Drew, wanted to help once it was known that Mrs. Delaney's husband was dying.

Kelsey arrived home after practice actually anxious to get to her computer. She needed to type the proposal into her word processing program, center a few lines, add a bold heading, include the list of deeds her classmates had promised, and it would be done, ready to place into her teacher's hands tomorrow before school.

First, though, she wanted to tell Russ they'd found a solution, that soon this mess would be over.

Gotta do better at thinking for myself, she thought as she waited for the computer to boot up. Even though the frustration that had led to the protest was real, it had been wrong to follow blindly along without getting all the facts.

Quickly she logged on to AOL, only to find the all-too-familiar e-mail waiting.

```
Envelope #2 is on Daddy's desk. Open it if
the protest did not end. Please record the
time.
```

Russ wasn't on-line. Kelsey checked the clock, responded with the time, and picked up the phone. Her sister-in-law answered on the fourth ring.

"Hey, Amy. How are you doing?" Kelsey asked, glad to hear a familiar voice.

"Apparently better than you. Russ know you're calling?"

Kelsey smiled. It was a rare day when Amy didn't look out after her husband's interests.

"No, but I need to talk to the old bear, and he doesn't answer his computer. Is he in the shop?"

"He's not an old bear." Amy bit off each syllable defensively, and Kelsey frowned. The whole family called Russ a bear when he was grumpy. The words weren't meant as an insult, only as a tease. Kelsey searched for another approach, but Amy made the first move.

"Sorry," she said, breaking the silence. "I didn't

mean to be rude, but you've made my life miserable these last few days. I've never seen Russ this unsettled."

"About school?" Kelsey asked.

"No, something about a fifth envelope, but he's all closed up. Even Nathan can't get him to talk."

Kelsey considered the remark. Nathan, their quiet, logical brother, who never took no for an answer, unable to get Russ to talk? This was serious.

"Has he told you about the protest?" she asked.

"Suzanne did."

"Well, that's what I want to talk to him about. I think I've found a way to end it so everyone wins."

"That would be good, Kelsey Gene. Whatever is bothering your brother doesn't need to simmer any more than it has."

This *was* serious. Amy was not one to jump on worries. "So, is he around?" Kelsey asked. "Maybe I can cheer him up."

"No. He's on patrol."

"Oh," Kelsey said, disappointed. "Where?"

"I think he has the interstate tonight. Selma could tell you for sure." Selma was the dispatcher who kept up with who was where when.

"Think maybe he'd meet me?"

"Could always ask," Amy encouraged. Sounds of fussing broke out in the background. "Looks like the kids are at it again. I'd better go referee."

"Wait, Amy, one more question. Russ has been, well, distant lately. Do you think it's the protest?"

"All I know is that he's the same big brother you've had all your life, and he's determined to find some way to get your attention." One of the kids screamed. "Listen, I really gotta run. Love you."

A quick click ended the call. Kelsey sat with the phone in her hand, not ready to let go. She knew the scream had been Megan's, probably because Charlie was winning the fight, and she missed being part of their life. How long had it been since she'd had dinner, baby-sat, read a story to the kids? *Might as well go downstairs and see what's waiting*, she thought, finally hanging up.

There were a thousand places where Russ could have left the envelope, but none affected Kelsey as much as her father's office did. Of all the rooms in the house, it held the essence of his life: pictures, scrapbooks, memorabilia. Even his cologne seemed to linger. Russ had taken one plaque off the wall and set it in the middle of the desk, under number two.

Subtle, Kelsey thought as she stuffed the envelope under her arm and picked up the plaque. It was an award given by the school board to her father in appreciation of twenty years of dedicated service. That was longer than she'd been alive.

"Is there something you are trying to tell me, Russell, dear?" Kelsey said out loud, looking around the walls. She found the empty picture hook waiting by the door and rehung the plaque on her way out. Although she'd been in the room less than two minutes, she felt its weight. Sadly she slumped down on the stairs outside the office door.

"Thank you, Russell. I needed that like I need another big brother." She drew the envelope out and tore it open. "So let's see what you have decreed."

YOU ARE GROUNDED FOR A SECOND FULL WEEK.

Kelsey sighed, even though the news wasn't unexpected. Russ tended to issue his restrictions in pairs: two hours, two days, two weeks. And as much as she hated being confined, she could use the time to catch up with her schoolwork. She wanted to be able to present Mrs. Delaney's assignments, completely finished, as soon as she could after they reached a compromise, so she'd let other classes slide. A major science project was due Friday, and the final draft of her story was to be turned in no later than Monday.

Still, Kelsey thought as she trudged upstairs, *if*

he's up to two weeks now, what's next? Usually if grounding didn't work, Russ moved on to something more creative, for example, assigning her a work detail, like scraping and painting the shed or thoroughly cleaning the garage. Kelsey didn't even want to think of consequences three, four, and five, at least not until the protest was over. Then it was going to be fun to see what unpleasantness her brother's ingenious imagination had produced.

You could let him know about the proposal, her conscience nudged, *especially since Amy said he was so concerned.* Kelsey plopped down on her bed and grabbed the phone. Why not? It might make his night go better.

She dialed the number to the barracks and waited. The dispatcher picked up on the second ring.

"Hey, Selma. This is Kelsey Blackwell. I need to get a message to my brother, but it's not an emergency or anything."

"Sure thing, sugar." Selma was soft, southern, and everybody's friend. "I'll patch into his car and leave a note on his computer."

Great! Kelsey thought as she heard the dull clack-clack of keys. *Another electronic wall.*

"What do you want me to tell him?"

"Tell him I need to talk to him. Ask if I can meet him on his break."

Again the familiar sound of the keystrokes reported Selma's actions. "It might take a minute—no, here comes the answer now. Just like Russell to be on top of things. Oh, my-y-y. You two having a fight or something?"

"Sort of. Why?"

"Give me a second." Again Selma attacked the keys, and again they waited. "Sorry, sugar. He says he's busy."

"Were those his exact words, Selma?"

"No, but maybe he's having a bad night."

Or a bad week, Kelsey added mentally. "So what *did* he say?"

"When I told him his sister wanted to talk to him, meet him on break . . ."

"Go on. It's okay."

"He asked, 'What sister?'"

Kelsey bit her lower lip, barely able to stop herself from screaming, *Go to hell, Russell Garrison Blackwell. See if I care!*

But she did care—and Russ knew it.

"You want me to send another message?"

"No," Kelsey answered. "I appreciate it, though. Thanks, Selma."

"Sorry, sugar. Let me know if you need anything else."

Kelsey hung up the receiver and dug into her pocket, feeling her keys.

What sister? What sister? Why don't you look me in the eye and repeat that remark?

It took exactly seven minutes to drive out to the interstate and ease onto the highway. Traffic was thin this time of night, and Kelsey was a good driver. All she had to do was to go back and forth, on the straightaway, first one side, then the other, until noticed. She had all night if that was what it took, and if she made contact with one trooper, any trooper, Russ would know. Steadily she pressed the accelerator toward the floor, tingling a little as the Renegade came to life. How many passes would it take. Two? Three? She checked the mirrors and pulled into the left lane, still pressing down, down, feeling her pulse race as she gathered speed. If her stubborn, bullheaded brother thought he could get away with humiliating her in front of Selma, he was wrong.

"Come on, Russell," she said into the night as the speedometer passed seventy. "Let's see you ignore this."

26

one pass

Kelsey hadn't expected Dan. He exploded out of his cruiser and covered the few feet to where she stood by the Renegade in a matter of seconds.

"Empty your pockets," he demanded, brushing by Trooper Cedric Johnson, who'd made the stop. Dan thrust out his open hand and waited.

"Why?"

He spread his fingers open wider. "Either you do it, Kelsey Gene, or I will."

She squirmed around and dug into her jeans, pulling out a lipstick, tissue, and a comb from one pocket, some folded money from the other. She hurled them onto the pavement and turned her pockets inside out.

"There. Are you satisfied?"

"No. Walk." He pointed to a spot ten feet in front of the car. "Toe to heel, toe to heel."

"You think I've been drinking?" Kelsey squeaked.

"Have you?"

"*No!*"

"Then walk."

"Damn it, Dan. I haven't been drinking." She started forward, at first shuffling, then adding more spirit to her steps until her feet were pounding the ground in precise frustration.

"That's far enough."

Kelsey pivoted around. Dan was standing, hands on hips, breathing though his mouth as if he'd just finished giving chase. He motioned her back.

"Was she driving erratically?" he asked, keeping his eyes focused on her movement.

"No, sir, only fast."

Dan frowned sharply and again pointed first at Kelsey then at the ground next to him. She stopped on the imaginary mark.

"Was she wearing her seat belt?"

"Yes, sir. She had to undo it to step out."

"How fast?" Dan asked as if he were gathering facts for a report.

"Ninety-three, sir."

Kelsey saw the breath catch in Dan's chest and hang before he exhaled. She had no idea she'd been going that fast, though it was the last thing she'd admit out loud.

"Okay. I'll take over from here."

Johnson hesitated. "Blackwell said—"

"*I* said I'd take over from here. Do you have a problem with that?"

Surprise flickered across Johnson's face. "No, sir. Not if you'll square it with Russ."

Dan nodded, and Johnson turned away, his heels clicking against the pavement like a metronome ticking off seconds in the night. His cruiser was barely out of sight when Dan let loose.

"Ninety-three miles an hour? Ninety-three?" he shouted. The colored lights flashing from his cruiser gave the whole scene a surreal tone.

"It was on a straightaway, Dan. No one else was around, and I *am* a good driver."

His eyes widened with an exasperated glare. "Don't you dare try to justify this to me," he sputtered, opening the door and motioning for Kelsey to get inside. She scampered across the seat, and barely avoided getting squashed when he slid behind the wheel.

"All right, what's going on?"

Kelsey swallowed hard. "I wanted to talk to Russ."

"You wanted to talk to Russ?" Dan repeated as if trying to draw meaning from the words. "Did it ever occur to you to use the phone?"

"I called Selma. Russ wouldn't see me."

"Then you were purposely speeding?"

How could she make Dan understand? She was a good driver, and she *was* going fast, but she had never been out of control. Speeding made it sound as if she were endangering others, and she hadn't done that. She was just driving fast.

Finally she shrugged and pulled out the only word that seemed appropriate. "Sorry."

"Sorry? That's it?"

"I don't know what else to say." She'd never seen Dan so angry. "I wanted to talk to Russ, and I thought if he saw a speeding ticket, he'd—"

"—he'd kill you, Kelsey Gene. Where is your mind?"

Kelsey lowered her head and shrank down. "Dan, I said I was sorry."

"Why?"

"Because . . ." Kelsey couldn't go on. Her tongue felt tacky and dry.

"Because why?"

She shrank even more. "I don't know," she mumbled, closing her eyes. "I think it's because you're so angry."

It sounded stupid, but it was the truth. She heard the car door open and slam shut, rocking the cruiser in its wake. In all the years she'd known Dan, she'd never seen him like this.

Good thing it wasn't Russ, she thought, sitting up

a bit. *Dan's right. He* would *have killed me.*

"If," Kelsey said out loud, "he admitted he had a sister."

Oh, her conscience nudged, *he would have admitted it all right. What was I thinking?*

She watched Dan's back, still leaning against the window, wondering what was taking him so long. Why was he standing there doing nothing? Finally he opened the door and threw his arm back into the cruiser, motioning for her to crawl out.

"I'm due a dinner break," he said with little emotion. "About a mile up the access road, on the right, there's an Italian café called Cal's. You lead."

Kelsey nodded. Ten minutes later she was sitting, leg stretched across the seat of a booth, back pushed up against a window, as far away from Dan as possible. She knew that within seconds, as soon as he'd finished ordering, she'd have his full, albeit unwanted, attention.

"I'm not going to talk to the side of your head, Kelsey Gene," he said after the waiter left. "But I am going to talk. Now, or later."

She kicked her feet under the table and shifted forward, eyes stuck to her iced tea glass.

"Look at me."

She glanced up, then quickly away.

"Come on," Dan said, his voice sounding softer.

He took her chin in his hand and pulled her face away from her chest. "Try again."

It took every ounce of Kelsey's courage to hold her gaze, and if she hadn't caught a small hint of sympathy from Dan, she wouldn't have made it.

"If I know Russell, this will probably be the shortest lecture you've ever had, Kelsey Gene. I'm going to say two words, and then I want you to repeat them. Understand?"

She nodded. Anything to be done.

"Speed kills. Say it."

"Speed kills." The words were barely audible.

"Louder, please."

She cleared her throat. "Speed kills."

"Seven times. Say it seven times."

Kelsey repeated the syllables over and over, feeling them burn into her heart as Dan raised his fingers one by one.

"Think you can remember that?" he asked, taking her hand. Kelsey nodded.

"You know there is a device called a governor that sounds an alarm every time you go over a certain set speed. I could talk to Russ about having one installed on the Renegade." Dan's tone had changed from an insistent demand to a steady tease. "Or I could talk to Nathan about getting his friend Anthony to arrange for you to spend time in the ER. They always have an accident victim or two on Saturday night."

Kelsey stared down, waiting for him to be done.

"Or I could arrange for you to tag along after the next fatality when someone has to notify the family—"

"Or you could be quiet," Kelsey interrupted meekly. "You've made your point, Daniel."

"Have I?"

She nodded.

"Good. Now tell me what's up with you and Russ."

Two plates piled high with a sampling of a half-dozen tastes arrived before Kelsey could answer. Dan enjoyed out-of-the-way eateries with house specials. He had his favorites—this Italian café, a Chinese kitchen, a small country diner—and though at first Kelsey wondered how she would ever swallow even one bite, mouthful after savory mouthful soon warmed her empty stomach. As they ate, they talked, about Russ, the protest, the envelopes, until both declared they were too full for more.

"Tell me something, Dan," Kelsey said, pushing her plate aside with an almost painful sense of pleasure. "How can you drive a high-powered car like the Vette and never speed?"

Dan's dark eyes brightened. "I can't."

"Then why are you all over me?" Kelsey blurted.

"Because you broke the law. I use a track on Saturday morning, not the interstate on Wednesday night."

"Oh," Kelsey said, surprised. Why hadn't she heard about this before?

"Want to come with me sometime?"

It was as if he'd read her thoughts and were quietly offering an invitation to share more of his life.

"I could drive the Vette?"

Dan choked on his iced tea. "No way, but you can come along for a ride. I've taken it over one twenty on the straightaways, and it's awesome."

Kelsey gazed away and imagined the sound of the engine's protest as Dan downshifted for curves.

"You'd love it," he said, smiling at her dreamy expression, and Kelsey felt herself flush, something she noted happened rather easily around Dan.

She looked across the table. "Did you really think I'd been drinking tonight?" she asked, changing the subject. His initial reaction still stung.

"It never dawned on me you would purposely try to get Russ riled. I was checking out reasonable possibilities."

Kelsey shrugged. "What can I say? It wasn't the best decision of my life, but I am a good driver."

"Good or bad driver has nothing to do with this, Kelsey Gene," he said.

"I know." She agreed quickly. "Speed kills."

Dan smiled and nodded. "And do you also know that Russell loves you?"

The sudden shift in conversation startled Kelsey. "Of course I know he loves me."

"And that he probably is very unsure of himself?"

Kelsey frowned. Where was Dan going with this?

"That he may be more afraid of failure than you realize?"

"What failure?" Kelsey asked. It was the same old song. "If you're talking about his *duty* to Dad, then he needs to get over it."

"What I'm talking about is the fact that Russ loves you, and he doesn't want to fail you as a brother."

As a brother? she wondered. "What do you mean?"

Dan took Kelsey's hand in his. "You are very special to Russ, his only sister, and he has dreams for you, hopes. I'm not even saying these are defined in his mind, but they are there. Love. Happiness. Health. The things we all want for those we care about."

Kelsey nodded and waited for Dan to finish.

"I think he isn't sure what to do sometimes. On the one hand, he is your brother, but then he is your guardian. And sometimes one role conflicts with the other."

"How?"

"Well, brothers are more contemporaries, equals. They usually don't have to make parenting decisions. Russ does."

Kelsey sighed. "So what are you saying, Dan?"

"I'm saying that since your dad died, Russ has been traveling in new territory, where there are no maps or guidelines. And he's trying to be the best guardian-brother he can. You do know he loves you."

Tears welled in Kelsey's eyes, and she lowered her head as she nodded.

"Then maybe you need to trust that love a little more. Talk to him like a brother. Let him into your life. You two were doing so well until all this happened."

Again she nodded. It was something to think about—later.

Dan let go of her hands with a gentle squeeze and glanced at his watch. "Guess I need to get back on patrol," he said, laying thirty dollars on the table and motioning for Kelsey to get up. "You going to be okay?"

"Yeah," she said, giving him her best smile, forcing back the brief surge of emotions that threatened to put a damper on the night. "Where do you find these places anyway?"

"Russ found Cal's. It's a kind of tradition at the barracks to see who can locate the best eats."

They stepped outside into the crisp, clear night air,

feeling comfortable in the silence of their friendship as Dan escorted Kelsey to her car. He glanced around the lot and, when he saw they were alone, pulled Kelsey in for a hug. "Do you remember what I told you?"

"Speed kills." Kelsey sighed against his chest.

"Good," he said, giving her back a gentle pat before letting go.

Kelsey took out her keys. "So what are you going to tell Russ?" she asked, unlocking her car.

Dan opened her door and stood back. "I imagine I'll tell him the truth, Kelsey Gene. Johnson was waiting for your brother, not for me."

"Guess I'm lucky you got there first, huh?" Kelsey said sincerely. Meeting with Russ would have been a disaster.

"Guess you were lucky Russ was tied up on an accident. Judging from the few words he spit out over the computer, I don't think you want to see him for a while." Dan shoved the car door closed and pulled back. "I'll follow you to the freeway."

"You going to clock me?" Kelsey asked, turning over the engine.

Dan's eyebrows shot up, and she laughed out loud, revving the motor. "Seventy-five? Everyone goes seventy-five!"

"Not in a seventy-mile zone!"

"Then seventy-one?"

Dan shook his head as he walked back to the cruiser, and Kelsey grinned happily. She'd shared a wonderful meal with a good friend, and an end to the protest was near. What more could she ask?

Only that when Russ heard the details about tonight's escapade, he would be in one heck of a forgiving mood.

27

a personal warning

The hope Kelsey felt when she returned from seeing Dan stayed with her through the night. It had been only a slight break from the monotony of her own company, but it had been just what she needed to gather some spirit other than despair. She grabbed her bag, bounced down the stairs, and turned back toward the kitchen. A whiff of coffee brought a smile to her lips. Nathan must have forgotten to turn off the pot, meaning fresh brewed, not nuked. She stuck her head into the room and froze.

"I heard about your little stunt last night," Russ said, taking a step in Kelsey's direction.

"Well, I wanted to talk to you, Russell."

Move slow and easy, she told herself, trying to slip by casually. *Act like it is any other morning, as if every day you find your brother—*

Russ stepped into her path, bringing an abrupt

stop to her exit. "You want to see me? Then come to my house, to the barracks, whatever, but don't you *ever* take it to the highway again! Do you understand?"

Kelsey dropped her bag and nodded. Clearly Russ had been simmering for a while. There was nothing she could do but listen, and the sooner he got on with what it was he had to say, the sooner she could get to school.

Russ leaned back against the door and crossed his arms over his chest. "So what was so gosh-awful important that you risked your life to tell me?"

"I want to know why you've changed." It wasn't the original statement. She'd called Russ to share news about the proposal, but it *was* the root of the matter.

"Changed? As in how?"

Kelsey rolled her eyes. Answering a question with a question again, his favorite old trick. "As in I think you know how. We haven't had a real conversation in days."

"It looks to me like that's what we're doing now," Russ responded.

"No. This is not a real conversation at all. You're standing there like a trooper, and I'm getting chewed out. I mean a real conversation, as in, How is Amy? Work? The kids?"

"I see," Russ said. Without changing his expression, he stepped back and opened the door. "Let me know when the protest ends."

"Russell Blackwell, get back here!" she yelled to his back, but Russ kept moving.

"Looks like you got his attention, sis."

"Shut up!" Kelsey said. She had no idea how long Nathan had been standing behind her, but all she needed was one more brother paying her too much attention. He reached out his hand to squeeze her shoulder, and she shrugged him off.

"Hey," he demanded, "don't you dare turn your anger at Russ toward me."

Kelsey grabbed her bag. "Well, why didn't you say something, instead of just standing there watching?"

"Maybe because I'm exhausted, or maybe because I just had breakfast with Anthony, who lost a ten-month-old baby that he might have been able to save if her mother had brought her to him sooner." He paused and let the reality of his words grab hold. "And maybe, Kelsey Gene, because your problems with Russ are not the only things happening in this world."

"A ten-month-old baby?" Kelsey asked, stunned. Nathan nodded wearily. "What from?"

"Pneumonia."

"Oh, Nathan," Kelsey whispered, "Anthony must really hurt."

"Probably a little more than your pride because

your big brother chewed you out." He grinned a little when Kelsey rolled her eyes. "So why was he here?"

"If you must know, I got caught speeding last night," she answered, getting her travel mug from the dishwasher.

"How fast?"

Kelsey stopped. Nathan, who had heard too many stories from Anthony about putting people back together in the ER after foolishness on the road, wasn't going to be any happier with the number ninety-three than Dan or Russ.

"Then you deserved his reprimand, Kelsey Gene," he said, turning away. "Good night."

"Please don't be angry." *And please, please don't turn away too*, she added silently.

"I'm too tired to be angry, though I'm sure I will be after I've rested and talked to Russ. I don't know what childish game you were playing, but you know better than to gamble with your life. We'll talk about this later, after I've slept."

His voice trailed off as he headed upstairs, and Kelsey sighed at the prospects of still another lecture. Nathan wouldn't forget.

"Well, at least I don't have to worry about what Russ will do if he finds out," she said to herself. She poured coffee into the mug and snapped on the lid.

"Wonder what he's cooked up in envelope number five."

Whatever. The protest would be over before she found out, and with such a wild beginning the day could hardly get worse.

But it did. First, Mrs. Delaney was absent again, and although they agreed that until their teacher had clearly accepted the proposal, the protest should continue, tensions rose.

Then, much to her dismay, Ms. Elliot played someone else at second during the scrimmage—at second, Kelsey's position for the last six years! She protested, but the coach remained adamant, claiming she wanted to be prepared in case Kelsey missed the first game.

Never, Kelsey thought as she left the gym after practice. *Second base is mine.*

She looked toward the parking lot, a habit bred by Russ's careful training. *Always be aware of your environment. Notice who's around*, he'd say. Most of the cars left belonged to athletes: Marti's Geo Storm, Ratasha's Ford Escort, Dan leaning against Kelsey's Jeep Renegade.

Dan?

Kelsey's heart began to race. When would she ever be able to handle the unexpected without thinking someone had been hurt? But Dan seemed relaxed, unruffled, not like last night. She put on her best smile and waved.

"Speed kills, Dan," she yelled. "See? I remembered." Dan nodded in approval, and Kelsey glanced around. "Where's the Vette? You haven't messed it up before I've had a chance to drive it, have you?"

He gave her a quick, friendly hug. "You're not driving my Vette, Kelsey Gene, so get off it."

He reached into his hip pocket and pulled out a business envelope with the number three printed clearly on the front. "Russ asked me to give you this. Said to tell you he hasn't changed any of the consequences since Tuesday."

What a strange message, Kelsey thought as she toyed with the envelope, wondering what her brother would do if she simply refused to open it. She slipped her index finger under the flap and tore the top edge. No use testing the waters.

NO CAR WHILE YOU ARE GROUNDED.

"I don't believe this!" Kelsey yelled, crumpling the paper into a ball and slinging it across the lot. It danced in the wind, mocking her, refusing to leave as it swirled back to her feet. She stomped on it, twisting her ankle back and forth, grinding it into the pavement.

"That's why you don't have a car, isn't it? You're here to take mine!"

"Don't slay the messenger, Kelsey Gene," Dan said. "After this morning would you rather have seen Russ?"

She turned her back to him.

"I'm here as a favor to you both," he said, reaching around her arm and holding out his open hand.

She pulled her keys from her pocket and slapped them into his palm. "You're going to *have* to let me drive the Vette to make up for this, Daniel."

"No," he said. "I'm not!" He unlocked the door, and Kelsey crawled in.

"Seat belt?"

"Oh," Kelsey grumbled, buckling up. How easily things were forgotten when a habit was changed.

By the time they pulled up at her house, Kelsey had resigned herself to the inevitable. JJ wouldn't mind swinging by in the morning, and Marti could take her home after school. It would be tolerable, if inconvenient.

Still, she couldn't help wondering what Russ had planned next. Pulling out her fingernails? The rack?

Dan lowered the visor and pressed the switch on the remote control. The garage door slowly eased up.

"Need this?" he asked, pointing to the flipper.

"No. I'll use the keypad." The prospect of another sandwich and cup of soup flashed before Kelsey's eyes, and she sighed. "Want to come in? I'll fix you a hamburger."

"We both know you're grounded, Kelsey Gene."

"I won't tell if you won't."

Dan laughed. "Which is probably why Russ invited me over to dinner. Sorry."

Kelsey nodded and got out. It had been worth a try. She stopped by the open garage and waited, wondering what was taking him so long to leave. Dan turned the Jeep around, then looked back over his shoulder, as if he had something else to say.

"What?" Kelsey asked, puzzled.

"Russell's not saying much, but this protest really has him bothered." He stopped and thought a moment before continuing. "He won't let you go to a hearing, not before the very people who so respected your father. I don't have any idea what he's going to do, but I don't think he's bluffing."

Kelsey smiled. "I'd say thanks for the concern, but that's hard to do when you're driving off into the sunset with *my* car."

"You're welcome." Dan eased out the clutch and inched forward, waiting at the end of the drive for Kelsey to lower the door.

She punched the button on the garage wall and stood watching the emptiness fade into black, wondering if that's how her mother's mind dealt with reality, dimming it until it no longer hurt. If so, Kelsey knew she was sane.

She passed through the kitchen without bothering to stop. Who wanted to eat anyway? Or sleep? Or do homework? Or laugh? Who wanted to boot up the stupid computer and check for messages? Dan would tell Russ she was safe.

I don't think he's bluffing. Dan's words roamed through her mind like a haunting echo, and Kelsey obediently plodded upstairs to record her arrival.

The usual e-mail was waiting.

```
Check in, please.
```

```
It's 6:39, Trooper Blackwell.
```

She could tell by her buddy list that Russ was online, and he hated being called trooper unless he was in uniform and on duty.

```
Is Dan still there?
```

```
No, Trooper Blackwell.
```

Twice. How many times would it take?

```
Does he have the Renegade?
```

```
Yes, Trooper Blackwell.
```

Three times?

```
Once more and I'm on my way over there,
Kelsey Gene!
```

Aw, yes, the third time was the charm. Kelsey pounded the keys as she laid in her answer.

```
Is this what I have to do to get you to
admit you have a sister?
```

Russ's response was slow.

```
Check in again before bed.
```

Kelsey smiled a little as her brother logged off. She'd made her point, and he had made his. Without the Renegade she had no easy means of escape.

She tried to concentrate on her homework, start-ing with math, hoping that working with numbers would help her forget about words and sentences and bargains and offers. No such luck. Finally she gave up. Maybe if she got some rest, her mind would go blank; she could think better without so much clutter.

She hit the space bar on the computer and logged on to AOL. Quickly she typed in her message.

```
It's 9:30. I'm going to bed.
```

```
We missed you tonight.
```

Kelsey's jaw slackened. She was dumbfounded. She hadn't even noticed that Russ was on-line, and it was the first personal thing he'd said in days. She pressed for more.

```
You too?
```

Nothing? Oh, well, maybe his remark had been programmed to answer her check-in. She was reaching for the mouse when suddenly the screen blinked.

```
Me too.
```

Kelsey stared, wide-eyed, unbelieving. Such simple words, gently glowing, telling her he cared. Suddenly her stomach growled. Funny how five little letters restored her appetite. She bounded downstairs and checked out the groceries: cheese, green pepper, mushrooms, onions, tomatoes. She could make a veggie pizza. Nathan would probably fuss about the fat content, but he'd eat a piece, and maybe he'd sleep better too.

Me too . . . me too . . . me too. . . .

The words rambled through Kelsey's mind and settled into a corner, permanently, comfortably, lessening her fear. By the time she cooked, ate, showered, and tucked herself into bed she was almost walking in her sleep. If Mrs. Delaney was absent again tomorrow, Kelsey was going to have to make Russ give her a little more time. She was going to have to appeal to his sense of equity. He'd always been fair before. Why would he suddenly change?

28

envelope number four

Kelsey stood in the middle of the den, trying to talk herself into moving. A message on her computer had instructed her to check their mother's dressing room. If Russ knew how much she avoided that part of the house, he'd come over, set her down, and they'd be having one serious talk. Some things it was best not to mention.

"Okay, on the count of three," Kelsey coached herself. "You can do it! One . . . two . . ."

She took off and breezed into her mother's bedroom, trying not to notice the picture of her dad propped on the dresser or his favorite sweater draped over the chair or the twenty-by-twenty-four-inch family portrait hanging on the wall. An envelope rested against a jar of her mother's night cream, and she snatched it, then turned and ran back into the den, crashing into the doorjamb on her way out. She stopped and rubbed her bruised hip, surprised to find her breath coming in gasps. Maybe when all this was over, she would have to tell Nathan about the difficulty she was having dealing with physical reminders of her past life.

And maybe you could talk to Russ, Kelsey thought, heading back upstairs. *You, know, like he's your brother.*

Ever since her talk with Dan she'd mulled over his words. Was she thinking of Russ as a brother? Or as a replacement for her father? The answer wasn't clear.

She plopped down at her desk and, unsure whether she was dreading the punishment or the fact that this was number four, toyed with the envelope in her hand. Mrs. Delaney had been absent again, so things were at a stalemate. Kelsey asked Ms. Elliot to drop the proposal off at the Delaneys' home after school, and the coach had willingly agreed, but still, it was going to be a long weekend.

"Might as well get it over with," Kelsey said out loud, tearing the end off the envelope.

All of the other punishments had been simple phrases, a few words. This one was different.

Kelsey Gene,

These last few days I have tried to be patient,

but if you are reading this, obviously my first efforts to get your attention have not been successful. So, for your fourth punishment, I want you to write an essay explaining what you would do in my shoes. How would you get *your* sister to stop her involvement in this protest? I will pick the essay up Monday morning before school.

Love,

Russ

Kelsey read it twice before setting it down. She hated when he did this, figuratively making her pick her own switch, and the worst part was he'd learned it from their dad.

So what *would* she do in her brother's place?

"Visualize," Mr. Marshall always said. "See it in your mind."

Okay. She was thirty-one and Megan was seventeen and Russ and Amy—she couldn't imagine them dead. Russ and Amy were traveling in Europe, the way her mom and dad used to do, leaving Kelsey in charge. Megan had become involved in a protest at school, and there was no time to ask Russ and Amy for advice. Kelsey had to come up with something on her own.

Grounding hadn't worked. Kelsey had taken away her car. She had pleaded, ordered, instructed, beseeched, and still, Megan had insisted on taking part in the protest.

Kelsey sighed, trying to think of something else. What? Community service? A day at the old folks' home? There was no time. Unless something was effective, and immediately so, the school board was going to meet.

"Okay," Kelsey said out loud. "Let her take her chances with the board. It's her life. Maybe the lesson she needs to learn is that things don't always turn out well."

And what would you tell Russ and Amy? That you'd let their daughter, your niece, be kicked out of school? By a group that honored your father?

Kelsey bolted up and started to pace. "Okay," she said out loud. "I'll go to school, pick up her pen, jam it in her hand, and make her work."

Could Russ force you? Kelsey wondered. *In front of your classmates?*

No. So what then?

Kelsey was blank.

"Damn your hide, Russell Blackwell." She cursed. "I don't *know* what to do."

She threw herself onto the bed and pulled a pillow under her chest. This was going to be the worst punishment yet, because until she came up with some answers, her conscience was going to eat away at her all weekend, and she was already feeling grumpy.

So what does Mr. Marshall tell you to do if you get stuck? Brainstorm. Talk to others, like Nathan, Dr. Lawrence, JJ, Ms. Elliot. Kelsey stirred. It was worth a try, even if it was against Russ's rules.

In spite of her best intentions, though, she didn't have any more written on Sunday night than she had on Friday. Jim Lawrence had said he'd make Marti choose a consequence, then applauded Russ for doing the same. Nathan was absolutely furious about the speeding episode, especially when he'd heard she'd been going ninety-three. After listening to his lecture, Kelsey had wisely given him his space. Ms. Elliot had called to say she'd taken the proposal over to Mrs. Delaney's, but she didn't have any suggestions for the essay. JJ wasn't able to come to the phone. Dan, Amy, and Marti were all out of ideas too.

Kelsey would have to solve the dilemma herself, and Russ would be waiting in less than ten hours for her final draft. She picked up her pencil and a sheet of plain yellow paper and wrote one word: "Help!"

Then, as JJ had done on Wednesday, she drew a web from the word, filling in "who" ("Kelsey"), "what" ("Needs to end the protest"), "where" ("At school"), "when" ("Immediately"), "why" ("Because it's messing up her life"), and then she added "how." How? By picking up her pen tomorrow and doing the work! If it were that simple, why hadn't she done it before? Because she had been too worried about JJ and Terrance and the others?

Maybe. Maybe she *had* followed along too quickly, before she had known all the facts, acted before she'd thought things through. She never would have considered a strike on her own, so how was going along with her classmates showing independence? It wasn't, and Kelsey knew that it wasn't. It had been a lesson hard learned.

Now she had to pay the consequences for her actions, because until she got Mrs. Delaney's answer, until she heard that her teacher had accepted the proposal Kelsey had carefully drafted, she was stuck. She couldn't quit until she had some hope of restoring her grade.

So tell Russ that! her conscience urged.

No, what he wanted to hear was what she'd do if she were in his shoes, not an excuse for continuing the protest. And all she could do was tell him the truth.

She booted up the computer and began to type, slowly, thoughtfully. It might not be the answer Russ wanted, but it was the best she could provide. It took almost an hour before she finished. She'd written slightly over two hundred words, struggling with each and every one, but she felt satisfied with the final result.

While the document was printing, Kelsey pulled out a business envelope, addressed it to her brother, and drew a smile for the return. Then she carefully reread the essay. It wasn't great, but it spoke her heart, in her own unique way, and if Russ was the brother she thought he was, he'd understand.

29

day ten

The aroma of coffee gave away Russ's presence even before Kelsey started downstairs, and in spite of the early-morning pep talk she'd given herself, she felt shivery. There would be no other delays, no excuses. Everything that had happened over the last two weeks was coming to a head in the next eight hours. She took a deep breath, put on her best smile, and burst into the kitchen.

"Hey, Russ! How's it going?" she asked, trying to act as if this were an ordinary moment. She poured herself a big mug of coffee and slid onto the bench opposite her brother at the breakfast table.

"You have your essay?"

"It's upstairs," she answered quickly. "I'll give it to you later." She took a small sip.

"Go get it."

"Let me have a little more coffee." She held the mug to her lips.

"Nope. Now."

So much for conversation, she thought as she put her cup down and headed back upstairs. Her bag was packed and ready, sitting on the foot of her bed where she'd left it, hoping to avoid what was about to take place.

She went back downstairs and heaved it up on the counter. "You know, I'd rather you read this later."

"I know," Russ answered.

Reluctantly she pulled the envelope from the side pocket and placed it in her brother's hand. Then she picked up her mug and leaned back against the counter, smelling her coffee. No way could she swallow, but she needed something to steady her hands.

Russ studied the envelope before tearing it open, and Kelsey watched his face. She knew each word by heart.

Once upon a time there was a family of bears. There were two little bears, a medium bear, and three big bears. They lived together, but in separate caves, and the biggest bear of all, an old rugged grizzly, watched over them carefully.

One day the medium bear, who was perky and sweet, got into trouble at school. When the old grizzly found out he growled, and growled, and growled!

The medium bear wanted to be good, to do what

the old grizzly asked, but she also wanted to help her friends. She felt caught, and the old grizzly growled even more.

Then the medium bear came up with a plan. Her friends agreed that it was good, only the teacher didn't come to school, so they couldn't put the plan in motion. And when the old grizzly found out the medium bear was still in trouble, he growled so loud he couldn't hear anything over his own roar.

Finally the old grizzly, still growling, asked the medium bear what she would do if she were in his place. She tried to imagine. She thought very hard, but she wasn't big and old, she was perky and sweet. She had no idea what she would do.

So she told the old grizzly, who was wise and kind, that she trusted his decision, and everyone lived happily ever after.

"I see you took this seriously," Russ said, looking at her.

Kelsey groaned. "I did, Russ, really. I just couldn't come up with anything, but I really, really tried, real—"

"Hush, Kelsey Gene. You're babbling."

Kelsey stopped and lowered her head into her left hand. She was close to tears, and she didn't want to cry, not now.

"Nathan didn't have any ideas?"

Nathan? What on earth was he talking about? She separated her fingers and peeked at his face. Russ's eyes were twinkling!

"I understand you two had quite a little chat this weekend, something about your going ninety-three?"

"He's mad as a wet hornet, and you know it!" Kelsey shot back. The conversation was becoming bizarre. One minute her brother's temper was threatening to explode. The next, he was teasing. He got up and rinsed his coffee mug, then turned around and leaned back, inches from his sister.

"An *old* grizzly, Kelsey Gene?" he asked, looking down.

"You know, red fur? Huge? Protective?"

"But old?" he asked. The slow process of aging was a thorn in his side, and everyone in the family knew it.

Kelsey sucked in her cheeks as she pushed away from the counter, set her mug down, and picked up her bag. This was more like the Russ she knew.

"Well," she said, slowly inching toward the door, "you *are* old, *and* you're getting soft. Assigning an essay? You know I love to write. And letting me call you Trooper Blackwell what? Three times? There'd have been a day you'd have headed over after the first one, and without a warning either. But hey, I do appreciate the fact that your temper's settled down, Trooper Blackwell. I mean, getting old affects people in different—"

Russ started to move, and Kelsey bolted out the door, slamming it in her brother's face. He chased her around his truck twice before she cried uncle and stopped.

"Who am I, Kelsey Gene?" he asked, standing at her toes in his best trooper pose.

"My brother Russ." She tried not to laugh.

"Not Trooper Blackwell?"

She shook her head a little too seriously. "Maybe to some people, but not to me. To me you're my brother Russ."

"And am I old?"

Kelsey's eyes widened in mock concern. "If I say no, are you going to ground me for lying?"

Russ groaned in defeat as he escorted his sister to the passenger seat of the truck. "What am I going to do with you, Kelsey Gene?" he asked, and she smiled. It was almost as if things were normal.

On the way to school Russ narrated a wild tale about Megan, a sack of flour, and a two-year-old's decision to bake Daddy cookies. It had taken Amy a whole morning to clean up her child and the kitchen and had taken Russ the rest of the afternoon to restore his family to peace. Kelsey closed her eyes and saw Megan, covered in white dust, happily mixing away while the kitchen floor turned to a sticky paste. It wasn't until they had arrived at school and Russ had fully stopped his truck that he returned to the business of the day.

"You know, Kelsey Gene," he said, "I meant what I said when I told you the last envelope would end your involvement in the protest."

"How?" Kelsey asked, her mouth suddenly dry. She'd never for one second doubted that her brother was anything but serious.

He smiled a little. "That is something I pray you'll never have to find out. Have Marti drop you off at home. I'll meet you there."

Kelsey nodded and got out, for the first time noticing JJ perched on the steps leading to the girls' gym, quietly watching. She waved and stepped back, giving her brother room to pull away.

"How's Big Red doing today?" JJ asked as she settled down beside him.

"Today's number five," she said, "the envelope that ends all."

"And you still have no clue?"

Kelsey shook her head. "How about you? Your dad settled down any?"

A lopsided grin settled on JJ's lips. "Did I come to the phone when you called Saturday? In fact, did I come out of my room all weekend except to go to church? I'm pale from lack of sun, weak from lack of exercise, melancholy from lack of love."

Kelsey laughed. "You're a mess, JJ!"

A smile softened his serious scowl, and he laid a hand on her shoulder. "I'm glad you're happy now, because what I've got to say isn't exactly going to make your day."

Kelsey froze. Bad news this early only meant one thing: Mrs. Delaney was absent again. He didn't even have to say it.

A deep frown crossed her face. "I don't want to fail English, JJ. But we've got to know where we stand, whether we can make up the work."

"I know," he said, patting her back. "Mrs. Parks said she'll be here, but later. So we may not be able to talk to her before class."

Kelsey nodded, and the two sat quietly together, gathering calm from the early-morning breeze. A car pulled into the student lot, followed by another, breaking the sense of isolation that had settled around them.

"Did Mrs. Delaney say anything when Ms. Elliot dropped the proposal off?" JJ asked, reluctantly getting up.

Kelsey shook her head. "Apparently her husband was having a really bad day. Ms. Elliot didn't stay more than a few minutes."

"It is hard to go through something like that alone," JJ said, frowning. "Maybe she'll let us help."

"Maybe," Kelsey said, picking up her bag. "But one thing's for sure, I am not going to face Russ tonight without being able to tell him I talked to her, even if I have to go by her house after school."

"If it comes to that, I'll go with you," JJ said, nodding with approval.

The words settled on Kelsey's heart, and she smiled. Maybe this day would end on a good note. Maybe Mrs. Delaney appreciated the proposal and would let them help.

If not, well, then, Kelsey would just have to figure another way out of this mess. Grades or no grades, it was time for the protest to end.

30

an advocate

Kelsey stopped by English after first period, second, third, fourth, and fifth; Mrs. Delaney was nowhere to be found. Her coffee cup and satchel had appeared around ten, but it was as if she was purposely avoiding her AP seniors until class. Even when the tardy bell signaled the beginning of sixth period, she was conspicuously missing.

And the class was abuzz. They'd heard Mrs. Delaney was in school, and one way or another they were going to make her commit, yes or no. Either they could make up their work or not. But it was going to be settled.

And if she says no? If she won't let you make up the zeros?

Kelsey considered the possibilities. She could transfer out of AP into regular English. Ratasha had heard of a night class that was starting next week, and

JJ had come up with a course being offered on the Net. Most likely they could pass the credit by exam test for regular English, so there were ways to graduate with their class—if they didn't get expelled.

They hoped, though, that Mrs. Delaney *had* understood their underlying message. They really wanted to help.

The thump of hard-soled shoes sounded, coming down the hall, louder, louder, slowing, turning.

"Okay, class," Mrs. Delaney said as she entered the room through the back door, "today I'm going to present an overview of the term *censorship*, including the structure of common arguments on why, under certain circumstances, books should be banned. We shall also look at opposing views, at reasons why many consider censorship unconstitutional. Then, after we have discussed the basics, you will each choose a book from a selected list of titles that have been banned somewhere in the United States within the last five years. You must have this book read by next Monday, at which time you will take a position and defend it to the class. You will be assigned to prepare for pro or con."

Kelsey's mouth flew open. A novel by Monday? Debate? Mrs. Delaney reached the front of the room and spun around, staring in exaggerated surprise at the empty desktops.

"What? No pencils? Paper? I thought you wanted to learn! Kelsey, would you please take the roll? The form is on my desk. And, Terrance, please lower the screen."

There was a general scrambling. Kelsey and Terrance jumped to their assigned tasks, while others got out supplies and settled in to take notes.

"Thank you. Now where were we?"

For forty-eight of the next fifty-two minutes, Mrs. Delaney taught, diagramming the structures of persuasive argument on the overhead, modeling sample rebuttals, and finally presenting the book list for the independent reading. By the time she concluded her lesson and leaned against the chalk tray to watch her students pack up, Kelsey's hand hurt from writing so fast, but it was a good sensation.

In less than a minute binders were closed, books stacked, and a low chatter had spread through the room. Mrs. Delaney straightened up and stepped forward, clearly expecting quiet.

"The last two weeks have been painful for me, as I am sure they have for you," she said, slowly measuring her words. "Perhaps we've both learned lessons in communication and trust. Perhaps I should have told you about my husband." For a brief moment she teared up but reclaimed her composure immediately, as if she were accustomed to the need for quick recovery. "And perhaps you could have told me your concerns instead of taking matters into your own hands. I would have listened."

She took a deep breath and went on. "I have spent the better part of the morning taking steps to call off the hearing. I have also placed packets of the work missed on the corner of my desk. You have two weeks to do the make-up assignments. The zeros for quizzes and tests will be dropped."

She glanced at the clock and hurried along. "It's never been my way to discuss personal problems with students, but since you now know about my difficulties and since you have offered, I shall appreciate whatever time you can spare. There is a clipboard on the file cabinet listing things I need. And," she said, inhaling deeply for a second time, "thank you for your concern."

The bell rang right on cue, and Mrs. Delaney headed quickly to her desk, brushing a few stubborn tears from her cheeks. She sat down heavily but managed to smile at each of the students as they picked up their work and eagerly signed up to help. Ratasha and Kelsey hung back, waiting until the others had left before stepping forward and pulling out their manila folders, which they proudly placed in the middle of the teacher's desk. Mrs. Delaney thumbed through

Ratasha's, which was on top.

"Ms. Elliot is a good friend to you girls," she said, looking up. "I'll have these graded in a few days."

The two hesitated, unsure if they should say more, then turned together toward the door.

"Kelsey?"

She looked back. "Ma'am?"

"I'd like a word with you, please."

Ratasha waved a quick good-bye and joined JJ, lingering in the hall.

Mrs. Delaney patted the chair by her desk. "It's okay. I'll write you a pass." She rested her arms on her lap. "Your brother dropped by my home yesterday. Did you know that?"

Kelsey shook her head. Nathan had been out for a few hours during their feud, but she hadn't asked where he'd been, and he hadn't offered any information.

"He brought me some fruit, and we talked a little while, about this and that. Then he asked me straight out to drop the zeros. It was clear that was his purpose in coming by, but, though I didn't tell him, I'd already made up my mind. Your proposal was so well written and full of goodwill, how could I refuse?"

"Nathan's always been a peacemaker," Kelsey said, wondering why he hadn't told her what he'd done.

"Nathan?" Mrs. Delaney repeated, wrinkling her

forehead. "Oh, Nathan Blackwell. I guess I never put you two together until now." She looked at Kelsey's hair. "It wasn't Nathan; it was Russell who stopped by."

"*Russ?*" The outburst turned several heads.

"You seem surprised," her teacher said, grinning at the reaction, "but you shouldn't be."

More like dumbfounded, Kelsey thought.

Mrs. Delaney picked up a pad of passes and began filling one out. "Russell's always had a big heart," she said, posting the time, "though knowing his reserve, I doubt it was easy for him to do what he did." She stood and held out the pink slip. "He really does care about you."

Kelsey nodded as she took the pass, her mind swirling from the news. Russ interceding on her behalf?

Still, one more thing needed to be said before she left.

"Uh, Mrs. Delaney, we're all sorry this hurt you. That was never what we meant. Thanks, you know, for giving in."

Mrs. Delaney leaned down and whispered into her pupil's ear, "Thank you for giving me an honest way out!"

With that she scooted behind Kelsey's chair and took off for the front of the room, leaving her student to be up and on her way.

31

endings

Kelsey stood in the kitchen, waiting, thinking through what to do next. All afternoon her conscience had plagued her, asking her why she'd allowed the protest to go on and on and on. Peer pressure? No, she'd stood up to her friends on bigger issues, and the concerns behind the protest had had validity. So why then? As a statement to Russ, to prove she was in charge of her own life?

I'd like to think I'm above that, she thought. *I know he trusts me.*

So why then?

Because you didn't think things through.

"That's it," she answered herself, though that lesson could be addressed on another day, another time. The question for today was, Why had Russ withdrawn?

The sound of her brothers' laughter wafting in

from the den warmed Kelsey's soul, and she stepped into the room.

"Hey, sis," Nathan said, giving her a quick smile.

Both brothers were sitting on the sofa, behind a virtual feast spread out on the coffee table. Buffalo wings, ribs, potato salad, beans, corn and rolls surrounded a cake with the words *It's Over!* written in blue on a pale yellow background. Matching party napkins and plates were on one end table, and a bouquet of balloons was tied to another.

"How'd you find out?" Kelsey asked, putting her hand on her stomach, which was growling in anticipation.

"Let's see," Russ said, leaning over and handing Kelsey a plate. "Jim, Suzanne, Sonya—"

"Terrance's mother?" Kelsey asked, surprised.

"Uh-huh. He called her right after class, and she said that since we'd shared the bad, we should also share the good."

Kelsey nodded, wondering where to begin filling her plate. It all looked so good.

"But that wasn't all, sis," Nathan said, waiting until his siblings had made their selections before starting on his own.

Russ laughed. "Kelsey Gene, I got so many calls today that Selma was ready to give me the dispatch desk. I may not have had your attention, but I sure had everyone else's."

"What on earth made you think you didn't have mine?" Kelsey asked. She grabbed a lap tray and sat down, looking around for something to drink.

"Maybe because in spite of his best efforts," Nathan said, holding up a bottle of Évian, "it took you two weeks to work things out."

Kelsey nodded, and he tossed her the water.

"Just because it took some time doesn't mean I didn't hear what Russ was saying." She dug her fork into the potato salad and savored the first bite, then looked at Russ, who had settled into the overstuffed recliner to enjoy his own meal.

"Thanks," she said. "This is great."

He smiled with pleasure.

"And thanks for going to see Mrs. Delaney too."

He pulled the fifth envelope out and put it on the arm of his chair. "I didn't want to have to give you this."

Kelsey eyed the envelope, the dreaded consequence that would have ended all. "Still, it was pretty special, what you did."

"You know, sis," Nathan chimed in, "Mrs. Delaney said it was your proposal that allowed the protest to end in a positive way. You did a good job negotiating."

It was that word again. "Dad would have been proud."

"Nathan." Kelsey put down her fork and took a long drink of water. "Why is it I think you have some point you're going to make here?"

Nathan shrugged sheepishly, and Kelsey grimaced. She should have known. She'd assumed the final words about the protest would come from Russ, but it was as if her brothers had a hidden agenda, some plan.

"Okay. What is it?"

"Do you think your feelings about Dad influenced how you acted these last two weeks?"

Kelsey looked at Russ. "I think you are talking to the wrong sibling here. It's Russ who needs that question."

"Why do you say that?" Russ asked, gnawing at a rib.

"Because you are so afraid that if you let up on me, I might make a mistake and that would mean somehow you failed Dad."

He dropped the bone and looked at her, startled.

"You forget that I'm seventeen."

"Kelsey Gene," Russ said, "I could not let you walk into that boardroom and face a hearing. I had to do something."

"Okay, but why did you withdraw from me?" There, the question was out for all to hear.

"Sometimes the only way I know to deal with life

244

is to step back a little to gain a balanced perspective."

Kelsey looked up, her eyes full of pain. "So you made a conscious decision to walk away?"

"Actually, no. Initially I wanted to give you some time alone to think, and I needed the distance too." He leaned back a little and ran his fingers through his hair. "I didn't want to act rashly, or I would have had to put up with Nathan's nagging. You have no idea how many times he's pleaded your case."

Nathan, who was listening intently, glanced quickly at the ceiling, and Kelsey grinned at his feigned innocence.

"Okay, so you needed some distance," she said, focusing again on Russ. "But two whole weeks?"

"After we got started, well, things kind of happened."

"Like the protest?" Kelsey asked, hoping to gain sympathy.

"Hardly. I simply noticed my withdrawal was making you squirm when nothing else worked. *I* wasn't acting out of stubborn pride."

So much for understanding. "Well, do you think you could at least agree that the next time you feel the need to step back we could sit down with Dr. Krammar or our strange-looking brother over there and talk things out?"

"Does there have to be a next time, Kelsey Gene?" His voice was quiet, plaintive, seeking deeper motives, and she sighed heavily.

"You being you, and me being me, I don't see how we can avoid it."

A slow smile of satisfaction settled over Russ's face. "You know, I think you *are* finally growing up."

Finally? Kelsey didn't know if she'd been complimented or not, but she blushed anyway.

"But for the record, next time I'm going to shave your head and make you wear sackcloth."

"Just don't go away."

"You mean, you'd rather I grounded you? Or took away your car? Or gave you a work detail?"

Kelsey nodded slightly. Where was he going?

"And what got your attention this time? One of the above? Or my stepping back?"

Kelsey shrugged. No way was she going to comment on that one.

"So are you over your inclination to sit in class doing nothing?"

"Are you over your inclination to issue envelopes with numbers on them?"

"For now," Russ replied. "Did you really draw a blank about what you'd do in my shoes? Or were you begging the issue with your grizzly bear story?"

"I had no idea."

"Me either."

The words danced around Kelsey's ears in a maddening whirl.

"You mean number five was empty?" she asked.

Russ glanced at her. "What do you think?"

"I've never in my life known you to bluff over something like this!"

"It isn't empty," he said, grinning at the absolute conviction of her words.

"Then what are you saying?" Kelsey asked, still perplexed.

"That I don't know if I could have gone through with what I wrote for the last consequence."

"So what was it anyway?"

"What was what?"

"The last consequence."

"I thought you ended the protest."

"I did, but—" Surely he wasn't planning to keep the contents secret, not after two weeks of worries and nightmares!

Russ picked up the envelope from the arm of his chair and studied it. "Nope. You haven't earned the right to see inside."

"I most certainly have," Kelsey insisted, pushing back and setting her tray aside.

Russ slipped the envelope under his shirt. "Not if the protest ended."

"You're saying I can't see inside?"

"That's exactly what I'm saying."

Kelsey lunged for his shirt and grabbed a handful of material. Instantly his hands flew out and caught her by the wrists. "Now, now," he said, squeezing until she let go. "After all the grief you've caused me these last two weeks, I think I'll hold on to this awhile."

Revenge?

No, Kelsey thought. *He's holding his trump card in case he needs it—next time.*

The tip of the envelope stuck out of his shirt, beckoning, calling. The other notes had been written on the computer. Maybe the next time she baby-sat she could hunt around his directories until she found the backup files and—

"It's not there," Russ said, releasing her with a final squeeze.

"What?"

"I wrote number five by hand. It's not in the computer."

Kelsey sighed. She'd gotten so used to Russ's sixth sense she didn't even question anymore how he knew her thoughts.

"But tell you what, Kelsey Gene," he said, smiling

a little too much. "Someday we'll open it together, just you and I, maybe the day you're married, or when your first child is born, who, by the way, I hope is a red-headed boy. Until then I'll keep it in a file folder in my desk."

Kelsey eyed him steadily. He was baiting her. He never locked his desk.

"How about after graduation?" she asked.

"Oh, that would be way too soon. And if I ever find out you tampered with this," he said, patting his shirt, "you'll have to accept what's inside as your punishment."

"You'll never know it's been touched," she declared.

"Bet me! And I'd never trust you again."

Kelsey groaned. She might risk losing a privilege or being assigned work or any of the other zillion things her brother could think up, but she'd never jeopardize his trust.

And Russell knew it!

Kelsey pressed her lips together, hard. What was it JJ had said? Consider what the opponent wants and what you have to give. So what did Russell want?

For you to get good grades and stay out of trou-ble, she told herself, but those things were not nego-tiable. They were expected. So how about a new tool for the wood shop? No, that would seem like a bribe.

Put yourself in his shoes. What would you want? She thought hard. He and Amy were always grumbling that between their careers and the children they had little time for each other.

That's it! Kelsey thought. *I'll trade places with them some weekend when Nathan is busy, give them the house while I watch the kids.*

The idea settled into her mind and found a comfortable niche. She could start out slowly, hint at how wonderful it would be if Russ and Amy could get away, let the idea gel, then make her money-saving offer: Since going away was so expensive, she'd trade places with them once a month until fall. That would give them five or six weekends of peaceful solitude. How could they resist?

And her price? Russ had to agree to let her open number five—without penalty.

She caught his eye, and again he slowly patted his shirt. Kelsey smiled and nodded, accepting the challenge. One way or another she was going to know what was inside that envelope.

The competition had just begun.